FIGHTING FOR MAGNOLIA

Redemption Harbor Security Series, Book 4

Katie Reus

Cover art by Sweet 'N Spicy Designs
Editor: Julia Ganis
Proofreader: Book Nook Nuts
Author website: www.katiereus.com

DEDICATION

For my sister, one of the best moms I know.

CHAPTER 1

17 years ago

Magnolia stared down at the incoming text message, following the one she'd just sent to her boyfriend. *Undeliverable*. Frowning, she called Ezra.

"We're sorry, the person you are trying to reach is no longer reachable at this number. Please try again later."

Ice chilled her veins as she listened to the automated message. Feeling panicked and trying to convince herself this was a mistake, she called again. Got the same message.

Staring out the windshield at the park where kids who were off school for spring break were playing, their parents watching, she tried to understand what was happening. Then she called Mari, her best friend.

"Hey, what's up? Did you tell him? What did he say? Do you want me to come over? Or kick his ass?" Mari Kim had two modes, kick ass and kick ass.

Magnolia was pretty sure she was going to take over the world one day. Or at least their little part of it in New Orleans.

"His phone is disconnected." At least her voice didn't shake as she got the words out. "And my texts were undeliverable. I...don't know what to do."

"Come pick me up now. We're going to confront him in person."

"Wait, I thought you were leaving today."

"No, my mom moved the flight to tomorrow morning. She has a meeting she couldn't miss. Now come pick me up."

A dozen excuses flittered through her brain, but she found herself, saying, "I'm on my way." Because Mari was right. Her bestie always pushed her out of her comfort zone, and ninety percent of the time she was grateful for it. Okay, ninety-eight percent of the time.

Magnolia didn't even remember the drive to her friend's house, but it wasn't like she had far to go anyway. They both lived in the Garden District with their parents and she'd only been at a park a couple miles away.

Waiting for her boyfriend to show up.

Before she'd even fully put her car into park, Mari slid into the front passenger seat, dumping a huge purse in the footwell. "I've got backup in case we need it."

She blinked. "What kind of backup?"

"Well...his neighborhood kinda sucks so I brought a Taser and bear spray."

"I don't even know what to say to that." To be fair, Mari wasn't wrong. She'd gone to Ezra's neighborhood once to pick him up (she'd wanted to see where he lived!) and he'd freaked out.

Or his version of freaked out, because he was always so calm, even when upset. But he'd been so adamant that she never *ever* come back there in case he wasn't there.

"I don't know..."

"You don't know what?" Mari turned in her seat to face her as the engine idled. Her long, dark hair fell over her shoulder in sleek waves. It was so dark that it almost looked blue-black in the right light.

"If we should just ambush him." And okay, she was feeling really vulnerable right now. They'd had big plans to move in together when they turned eighteen and now he just wasn't answering his phone. Or more accurately, his phone was disconnected. And she had no idea what to think.

"Oh." Mari strapped in now. "We're going. You're going to tell him you're pregnant, and then we'll tackle telling your parents. Unless you decide you don't want to have—"

"Nope."

"Okay, then. Let's go. Unless you want me to drive your car?" She shot Magnolia a sly look, her grin mischievous.

Magnolia just snorted and reversed out of the driveway. Mari had gotten her car taken away for like the fifth time when her parents had caught her sneaking out. *Again*. It wasn't like she'd been sneaking out to a party. No, her friend had been sneaking out for her part-time job. But her parents had a very clear vision for their daughter's future: Go to school. Become a doctor. Take over the world.

Magnolia was surprised they didn't realize Mari was going to do exactly what she wanted, whether they approved or not, but Magnolia's own parents didn't understand or know her either. Whatever.

"So how are you feeling?" Mari asked once they hit the highway, heading away from the downtown proper.

Ezra lived about half an hour away, wasn't even technically in New Orleans. But the drive wasn't far and she'd drive anywhere to be with him. "I don't know, honestly. Freaked out, I guess."

"I meant like...are you nauseous or anything. Because my halmeoni has a special tea if so."

"Oh my god, you told your grandma?"

"What? No. I just meant that she has a special tea for nausea. I remember my mom taking it when she was pregnant with my brothers."

"Oh, okay. And I feel fine." But she'd taken eight pregnancy tests and they were all positive. She wanted to go to her OB but wasn't sure if her doctor would tell her parents since she wasn't quite eighteen yet. Only one month to go. And at least she'd be graduating high school next month so she wouldn't be showing at her graduation. "I'm trying to figure out how I'll deal with college and...just, everything."

"You'll live at home instead of the dorms. Or you and I can just move in together."

"You're not going to want a baby for a roommate," she murmured as rain burst from the sky, drenching her car and the six-lane highway. She slowed, along with everyone else, almost grateful for the delay in getting to Ezra.

"Whatever. We'll figure it out. And luckily your due date should be right around December which means that if you have decent professors, you can take your exams early if the baby comes early. And if not, it's the perfect time for winter break."

She glanced at Mari in shock. "Clearly you've given this some thought."

"Well, I know you haven't. And I can't help it, it's the way my brain works." She popped a piece of gum in her mouth. "No matter what, you know your parents will support you. Your dad can be a dick, but your mom's the best."

"Thank you for being such a great best friend." She reached across the center console, took Mari's hand and squeezed.

Mari's dark eyes widened in surprise. "You don't have to thank me for that. You're always there for me."

"Since kindergarten." They'd gotten put next to each other for nap time, and had become best friends over their love of Pokémon trading cards. Her gut tightened as she steered onto the exit, the rain starting to fade now.

These April rains left as quick as they came so now she had no more excuses not to stop. Well, other than Ezra ghosting her. But no, no way. "He wouldn't just ghost me," she blurted, wondering if she was lying to herself. She hadn't talked to him in two days but they were supposed to meet up today so she'd thought…she didn't even know.

"I don't think he would either." But Mari bit her bottom lip, worry on her gorgeous face.

"But what if he is ghosting me? What if he's just done with me?" she whispered, voicing the fears she'd been trying to keep buried.

"Then screw him," Mari snarled, all righteous indignation. "You've got family and me. And I'm family anyway."

"Okay."

"Okay." Mari nodded once, the tenseness back in her expression as Magnolia made a turn at the next light.

Everything around here had an almost industrial, deserted feel to it. Some of that was from Hurricane Katrina almost two years ago. Her own neighborhood had only finally finished repairs and restorations at the end of last year. But the state hadn't put money back into some areas, including this one. And she hated that for Ezra, hated everything about his home life.

He'd told her some of it, but... "That's a For Sale sign," she murmured, nodding even as she slowed in front of the little teal house with peeling paint. A chain link fence ran the front of it, the weeds and grass overgrown in the small front yard.

"Park in front of his neighbor's curb." Mari indicated toward the white woman sitting on her front porch, smoking a cigarette. "I'll stay in the car in case someone tries to jack it. You take the Taser, I'll keep the bear spray."

Magnolia looked around the quiet neighborhood, didn't think anyone was watching them, but she also knew Mari was right. Even as she questioned everything, she parked, kept her little BMW running—a gift from her parents on her sixteenth birthday—and slid out of the car.

"Here," Mari held out a fifty. "Offer it in case she won't talk."

She blinked, but quickly shoved the money into her pocket. Mari always thought of everything. Half smiling, she approached the woman on the porch.

"I don't know nothing about that house for sale," the woman rasped out.

"Oh, no, I'm not here about that. Ah...do you know what happened to the people who lived there?"

The woman's eyes narrowed. "Why?"

"I'm friends with Ezra. We both work at the community center over in the Quarter. I haven't heard from him in a few days and I just got worried." She shoved her hands into her shorts, trying to cover the trembling in her hands. It wasn't a lie.

The woman's body language shifted as she shoved the butt of her cigarette in the cracked ashtray, then pulled out another one, lit it. "Oh, now that's a good boy. Real good. He always mowed my lawn when he was around. His father, if you could even call that sorry excuse for a human a father, is another story." She snorted, which turned into a cough.

Magnolia had to stop herself from peppering the woman with questions, was glad it was just her here and not Mari. Because she didn't think her bestie would be patient. She cleared her throat. "Do you know where he is or if he's okay?"

"Oh, he'll be fine. He joined the Marines, signed up yesterday. Told me he'd be shipping out soon. I guess they're sending him to Pendleton." The woman shrugged, took another drag. "Not sure what happened to his daddy, but hopefully he fell in a ditch somewhere and never got up." She laughed at her own words, took another drag.

"He's leaving?" she asked, more to herself than the woman as she tried to process the words.

"That's what I said isn't it? Now get out of here. No sense in you driving that car around here if you don't want it stolen."

Simply nodding, she turned back to her car, saw two men across the street watching her. Hurrying, she jumped into the driver's seat and pulled away even as she strapped in. "The woman said he joined the Marines."

"Wait, *what*?" Mari demanded. "Ezra did? What else did she say?"

"He's leaving, I guess. Heading to California." And she felt positively numb. "I don't even know how to get ahold of him." And she still couldn't believe he was just leaving her behind, hadn't told her he was going. Nothing. He'd been her first everything and she loved him. And she'd thought they were friends on top of everything else.

"We'll figure it out."

"Yeah," she managed to get out. But she wasn't sure she believed it at all. No, she didn't believe anything would ever be okay again.

CHAPTER 2

Present day

"So when are you and Fleur tying the knot?" Ezra asked as he and Tiago paused at the crosswalk.

"No way, not changing the subject. Seriously, how the hell did I not know you were from here? How have you not told anyone that?" There was a hint of hurt in Tiago's voice. "We've all been living here for the better part of the year. Not to mention I've known you for seventeen years."

"I'm not from *here* here." He shrugged, annoyed at himself for the slipup. He'd always told them he was from Ponchatoula, which was technically true. He'd been born there, but then his mom had died and his piece of shit dad had moved closer to the Gulf Coast for work. They'd ended up on the outskirts of New Orleans for a job his dad had managed to hold on to for about a year.

Tiago just grunted and looked away from him as they stepped up onto the sidewalk. They'd just finished a job and Tiago wanted to look at different homes. They were supposed to meet up with a real estate agent tomorrow, but he'd wanted to do some research on his own first, visit some open houses.

As they walked past a little vegan diner, then an old Victorian that had been turned into a bed and breakfast, his heart skipped a beat. They were way too close to some of his old stomping grounds.

To the home of the girl who'd broken his heart. The girl, now a woman, he'd never gotten over. No matter how hard he tried.

"I'm sorry, man," he finally muttered when it was clear Tiago wasn't going to talk to him.

Tiago stopped on the sidewalk, turned to face him, his expression surprised as he cupped his hand around his ear. "What? Can you say that again?"

"Man, shut up," he grumbled, nodding at incoming joggers.

He and Tiago stepped off the sidewalk as two women raced by them, expertly jumping over an uneven section in the cracked sidewalk where a magnolia tree root had busted up through the concrete.

"Oh no, I'm gonna need to hear the words again."

Ezra started walking again, knowing they were close to the address Tiago wanted to look at. There were a few places for sale around here so they'd parked and had been eyeballing the homes from the road. Some had walls, some fences and gates, and some just open gorgeous green yards.

Tiago fell into step with him. "One day you're going to have to accept that you're good enough, all by yourself."

Nearly tripping on absolutely *nothing*, Ezra shot his friend a sharp look. "What the hell are you talking about?"

Tiago shoved his hands into the pockets of his leather jacket as they approached a Queen Anne-style house.

And the only reason Ezra knew the type of architecture was because the girl he'd once been in love with had told him. She loved everything about this city and architecture in general. Which made sense since she'd been like third or fourth generation here and her parents had been rich as Midas from hotels and real estate. Something he wasn't going to think about. But being back in New Orleans was messing with his head. There were too many memories of her here.

He knew he should just look her up, maybe get a visual of her and get it out of his system. But he refused to do that. Not after the way she'd ended things. In seventeen years, he'd never looked her up.

Not after... Just not after.

He rolled his shoulders once, still waiting for a response from one of his best friends. He'd known Tiago since boot camp, had been lucky enough to be stationed with him in some of the shitholes of the world. And now they worked for Redemption Harbor Security, had just opened up a new branch in New Orleans, a city that desperately needed their help.

"You keep a little bit of yourself locked away from all of us, always have. And I know what I sound like right now and I don't care. I was talking about you with Fleur—"

"You're talking about me now?"

"Yep. Because I'm worried about you. And she's really insightful so I can't take credit for any of this, but she's right when she says that you always hold yourself apart. The fact that we literally just found out that you grew up here, not Ponchatoula, is basically Exhibit A."

"We're not in a courtroom."

"Whatever, you know what I mean. And I'm just saying that whatever bullshit voice in your head is holding you back from, I don't know, accepting who you are and where you come from, is a liar. You deserve all the good things that come your way and I hope you put down roots here."

"You sound like a shrink," he muttered, his friend's words striking far too close to the truth.

"That's not the insult you think it is."

"Oh my god, Tiago. I love you like a brother, but enough." He scrubbed a hand over his face as they approached the big *FOR SALE* sign in front of the pristine lawn. It was an open house and a couple were currently walking down the driveway, holding hands and smiling at each other.

"Fine, but I said what I said. And I mean it." Tiago held up his hands. "I'm done."

Ezra shoved out a breath, the tightness in his chest easing only a fraction since apparently Tiago was done. But he knew his friend, knew this wasn't over. "I'm gonna hang tight while you head inside."

Tiago looked as if he wanted to argue, but just nodded and strode up the long driveway to the pink and white two-story house. Ferns hung from the top and bottom porches despite it being December. It was a relatively mild one but still chilly enough to wear a jacket.

Which was a plus for him because it was easy to tuck away his pistol from sight, but still keep it close while working.

Two more couples walked out of the front door, laughing and talking to each other, so he turned away, headed back to the sidewalk. He should have just gone home today. Or to the condo he didn't think of as home. More like a place he laid his head at night.

He didn't think of anywhere as home. Never had. Though at one time he'd dreamed of making one with Magnolia.

But that was another lifetime ago. One he sometimes wondered if he'd imagined or dreamed up because his own life had been shit. No way had that year with Magnolia been real. But it had, and it had set the stage for everything in the future—and nothing and no one had ever compared to her. To the way she'd made him feel.

She'd seen him, the real him. And...he thought she'd accepted him.

He slid on his sunglasses as he made it to the sidewalk, mainly so he wouldn't have to make eye contact with anyone who happened to walk by.

A champagne-colored luxury SUV pulled to a stop on the curb when another car pulled away. Someone else coming to look at the house, no doubt. Someone had died inside it, so it was being marked down. That didn't seem to stop anyone, not in a city as purportedly haunted as this one. No, he had a feeling there would be a bidding war.

A woman with chestnut-colored hair stepped out and his breath caught in his throat. Then he ordered himself to calm down.

She was just a woman with dark hair. Not Magnolia.

But she had the same slim, elegant build. In fitted, dark jeans, four-inch heels and a short-cropped tweed jacket, she had her head down as she fiddled with something in her big purse. And all that hair was covering her face.

Jesus, the woman had no self-awareness. Sure it was a good neighborhood, but anyone could come up and rip her bag out of her hand, shove her back. Grab her keys and steal her car.

He glanced around, looking for any potential threats out of habit born long before he'd joined the Marines.

A dark SUV was slowly cruising down the cobblestone street, likely someone who lived here, was sightseeing or just wanted to see the house for sale. But then he saw it. Just a peek, but that was enough.

A suppressor slightly easing out of the driver's side window.

He didn't think before he moved into action, sprinting down the sidewalk in the woman's direction. "Get down!" he shouted even as he flew through the air, tackling her behind her SUV right as glass exploded around them.

Pop. Pop. Pop.

A giant potted plant nearby shattered, soil flying out everywhere as he covered the woman's body with his.

But he shoved up, withdrew his own pistol and aimed at the retreating SUV. The back passenger window shattered on impact and the driver took off, tires squealing as they escaped.

"Ma'am, are you—" He froze as he turned to find Magnolia pushing up from the ground.

"Ezra," she rasped out, big blue eyes blinking in pure shock.

He was aware of footsteps thundering their way, turned, ready to draw his weapon again, but stopped when he saw that it was Tiago racing toward him.

"I already called the police," Tiago said. "And told everyone to stay put inside the house."

He nodded, then turned back to Magnolia to find her simply staring at him, her face pale.

As if she'd seen a ghost.

CHAPTER 3

I'm really tired of life throwing me curveballs. How about some tacos instead?

Sitting in the office Detective Camila Flores had shoved them in, Magnolia tried not to sneak glances at Ezra Hunt.

Failed.

But he was staring at her too, so at least his shock was real.

"Are you sure you don't know who would want to hurt you?" Ezra finally spoke again, his voice the smoothest whiskey ever served. And he still looked the same.

Or similar, not the same. He'd turned into an even more attractive man. And that right there was an understatement. He'd been a boy, almost a man, and now he was all hard edges with the kind of arms that she wanted wrapped around her. Which wasn't that much different than before, but at least when they'd been seventeen almost eighteen, he'd had a little softness.

Looking at the man with the whiskey voice, amber-colored eyes, big, callused hands and gorgeous forearms she absolutely wasn't going to notice, she could almost swear she was falling back in time.

To a different place. When she'd been a different person.

A heck of a lot more fun, with fewer responsibilities.

Not that she'd change a damn thing, but looking at him almost hurt her physically. She glanced away, blindly stared at the dust-covered shelves. "I wonder where Camila found this office," she murmured, more to herself and definitely ignoring him. Her old friend had stuck the two of them in here, almost definitely to give Magnolia privacy. But she'd seemed to know or be acquainted with Ezra too. Which was weird.

Ezra shoved out a sigh, pushed up from this seat and started pacing in front of a desk stacked high with banker's boxes.

Yep, this place was definitely used for storage.

"So what are you doing in New Orleans?" she asked mainly to break up the quiet.

"I live here now."

Okay, that got her attention. After he'd tackled her to the ground, saving her from being shot—shot!—it had been a blur of noise, people, lights and sirens. Then they'd gotten back to the police department and been basically shoved into a dusty little room.

Out of the way.

When she'd been seventeen and scared of her parents' reaction, and her friends', she sometimes thought they wished they could shove her in a little room and forget about her. Or maybe she was simply projecting her fears from back then.

She pressed her fingers to her temple, lightly massaged. "How long have you been back?" she murmured, even though she told herself to curse him out for ignoring all her letters from so many years ago. For moving away without a word to her. As if she'd meant nothing to him. She told herself to give him the silent treatment the same way he'd done her.

But she wasn't built like that, and she was nervous. He was one of the few people who made her feel this way. Which just annoyed her even more. And being annoyed or angry was better than being scared.

"Not long."

Great. Fear punched through her because her past and present were about to collide. If she wanted them to. And right now she needed to talk to her best friend. Mari would know what to do. Her tornado of a friend always did.

"Magnolia, I feel like you're not taking this seriously—"

"Don't say my name." She whipped her head in his direction, long buried anger popping up. "You lost that right. In fact..." She'd stood, grabbed her purse, aka the thing that held her whole life, and made a move for the door when her son burst inside.

Eyes the same color as Ezra's were wide and panicked. "Mom!"

"I'm okay, everything is okay." She wrapped her arms around her son as he did the same to her, slightly lifting her off her feet.

In the last year he'd had a growth spurt and was now taller than her and had the body of a man. But his face was still her sweet boy's. Or maybe that was a mother's wishful thinking. "It doesn't sound okay. What happened?" He stepped back, looked at Ezra, frowned. "Who are you?"

"He's the man who saved me from—"

The door flew open again and a man with light brown skin and dark eyes strode in, looked between the three of them. Blinked when he looked at Lucas, then Ezra. Oh right, he'd been there on the sidewalk, the one who'd called the police. Tiago? Everything had been a blur, but she remembered him now.

"Ah, Detective Flores said I could come back. Rowan and Adalyn are on the way too..." He trailed off slightly, giving the two of them a look she was pretty certain she could read.

It was time to get out of here right freaking now. "We'll give you guys a moment of privacy." She grabbed onto Lucas's elbow.

Ezra stepped forward. "Magnolia, we're not done—"

She turned on Ezra. "We'll talk later," she snapped out before basically dragging her son from the dusty room and into the dim hallway.

A tall, broad-shouldered man and a strong-looking redheaded woman were barreling toward them. Magnolia turned to her son, kept her voice low. "We're leaving right now and I need you to not ask questions until we're out of here. Okay?"

He looked like he wanted to argue because of course he did. He was a teenager and he was her son. "Fine."

She smiled politely as she and Lucas hurried down the hallway, didn't miss the look the redhead gave Lucas. So these were Ezra's friends or coworkers or whatever, and two of them had most likely seen the similarities between Ezra and Lucas. Or she guessed that was why they'd done double takes at her son.

It was the only reason that made sense, unless they were straight up weirdos. Which, she supposed they could be that too. And okay, now she was spiraling.

Get it together, she silently ordered herself. *Be calm and think.*

She was hustling down the hallway toward the elevator, realized that her son was actually slowing down for her because his legs were now longer. At that thought, a pang hit her right in the chest as she remembered when she'd had to shorten her strides for him. When he'd held so desperately on to her hand because he'd been afraid of going into kindergarten by himself.

That hadn't lasted long, and soon he'd been happy to go to school, excited to see his friends. But now everything was changing and apparently the world had decided to lob another grenade at her in the form of her child's father.

The man who'd long since abandoned them, then shown up only to save her from some nutjob. "I get it, universe. I screwed up in a past life and you're still punishing me," she growled as she punched the button, desperate to get out of here.

"You're talking to the universe at large now?" Lucas's tone was dry, though she could hear the tinge of worry in his words.

"How did you find out about this?" Because she hadn't called her parents, hadn't called anyone.

"Miss Jessica told Vanessa, and Vanessa texted me."

Oooh, right. She'd been on her way to her friend Jessica's house for a quick visit when everything had gone to hell. "I was going to tell you, obviously, but I didn't want you to miss anything important at school."

"I didn't miss anything," he muttered. "And who cares about stupid tests?"

She bit back her response because of course he was concerned. She linked her arm with his. "You're right. I should have contacted you but I didn't want you to worry. And there was nothing you could have done about this."

"Other than be there for you?" He patted her arm as they stepped out into the hallway. This one was a lot busier than the essentially deserted floor they'd just come from.

"All right, you're right."

"Do the cops know who…" He trailed off as Detective Camila Flores walked toward them, purpose in her stride.

Today her longtime friend and all-around badass detective was wearing dark blue slacks, a blue and white striped sweater and caramel-colored boots with thick soles that were probably good for kicking in doors.

"Lucas! How are you so tall now?" Camila pulled him into a quick hug as the three of them stopped in the hallway in front of the break room doorway. "Come in here." She pulled her son, then motioned for Magnolia to step inside.

Two uniformed officers were sitting at a table, eating sandwiches and not paying any attention to them.

"Am I good to leave?" she asked, because she needed to get out of here and far away from Ezra Hunt.

Camila's expression darkened slightly as she nodded. "Yes. But I don't like what happened. Especially with the threats you've been receiving."

"What threats?" Lucas demanded.

Magnolia winced. "We'll talk about this on the way home."

"But—"

"Lucas, why don't you go grab a bag of barbeque chips from the snack machine down the hall?" Camila asked.

"I'm not five anymore. You can't just distract me with food."

Camila arched an eyebrow. "Who says the chips are for you?"

At least that got a half laugh from him as he turned and headed out of the room, no longer all gangly arms and legs.

"There's a vending machine in here," Magnolia murmured.

"Yeah but this one doesn't have the chips I like. And I wanted to talk in private. I know you've got good security at the house but I want you to make sure you've got your cameras always on, and set your alarm at night. And during the day too.

At least for now."

"Okay." Sighing, she dropped her bag on a nearby chair. "So do you have any news for me?"

"No. I've got a couple officers out canvassing, trying to see if anyone caught anything on their Ring cameras. You got really lucky with your Good Samaritan."

Lucky wasn't the word she'd use, but she simply nodded even as she fought exhaustion. "Do you think I'm safe to leave with Lucas?"

"Yes, but I'm going to have someone escort you home and we'll be increasing patrols in your neighborhood tonight."

"You don't need to do that. Save your resources. I've got a security system, cameras, and a gun if need be." She hated them, but still owned one and practiced at the range nonetheless.

Camila simply sighed, then pulled her into a quick hug. "We're going to get this guy."

Yeah, if they could figure out who he was—though she had a pretty good idea. And so did Camila. But finding the asshole was another thing entirely. Until today the threats had been messages left at one of the hotels her family owned and some with the receptionist of her firm. This had been a huge escalation and she could admit she was terrified.

She needed to talk to Lucas about everything, then convince him to move in with his grandparents for the time being. He wouldn't like it, but she didn't think he'd balk.

And more than that, she wanted to get him out of here before Ezra came looking for her.

CHAPTER 4

Ezra wanted to shove his friends out of the way and race after Magnolia, but took a deep breath. "Listen—"

"Are we gonna talk about the fact that the teenager who just walked out of here looks exactly like you?" Tiago asked, leaning against the dusty, box-covered desk, a bag of organic banana chips in hand. Where the hell had he even gotten those?

"Oh, thank god, I was hoping you'd say something." Adalyn snagged a banana chip from him, crunched away.

"Wait, what?" Rowan looked between Adalyn and Tiago. "What kid?"

"The one in the hallway with the brunette smoke show," Adalyn said.

"You're the only smoke show I see."

Ezra scrubbed his hands over his face, resisting the urge to run his head through the nearest wall. If he didn't stop them, they'd simply keep going. "You guys! That kid didn't look like me. She got married after we broke up." He'd gotten the wedding invitation, a nasty shove of a knife deep in his chest. Though she hadn't been wearing a wedding ring today, something he hated that he'd noticed. But screw it, if he was in the same vicinity as Magnolia Lavigne, he couldn't help but drink in everything about her.

She was even more gorgeous than he remembered and that should be impossible. Illegal. It was like the universe just wanted to kick him in the balls by showing him what he'd once had.

Adalyn and Tiago snorted in unison. "That *kid* is very likely seventeen, maybe eighteen. And he had your eyes," Adalyn added.

Ezra blinked. "He couldn't be eighteen..." But he could be sixteen or seventeen. *No. Just, no.* She'd have told him. Right? At one time he'd assumed she would have, then she'd coldly cut him out of her life as if what they'd shared had been nothing.

Which shouldn't have been a surprise really. Her family was one of the wealthiest in New Orleans, probably in the state and beyond. They'd been heavy into real estate, and whatever her father touched seemed to turn to gold. That, combined with her mother's family money—Abigail and Arnold Lavigne had been a power couple years ago. But he hadn't cared about any of that.

He'd just fallen for the dark-haired girl who blushed whenever he looked at her. God, she'd been so sweet and kind and nothing he'd ever thought he wanted. Or deserved. But...damn it, he wished he'd paid more attention to her son. He'd just been so entranced by her after all these years.

"That *was* Magnolia, right? *The* Magnolia," Tiago pressed.

"Wait, what! That was *her*? The one you used to mumble about in your sleep?" Rowan demanded.

Oh, he absolutely wasn't going to do this right now. "The only thing I want to talk about is the fact that someone definitely took a shot at her. That was not some random drive-by. That person was aiming for her. I'll meet you all back at the office." Because screw waiting for Detective Flores to come get him.

He slid past them out into the hallway, ignoring their footsteps behind him. Bypassing the elevators, he headed for the stairs and raced up them until he reached the right floor.

As he stepped out, he found Detective Flores waiting by the bank of elevators. "Detective."

She turned to him in surprise. "Mr. Hunt."

"Ezra is fine." Something he'd told her more than once. Since setting up shop here (and giving her a huge win by taking down a weapons- and drug-running asshole) he and his crew had worked with her on more than one occasion over the last year.

She was friendly with Adalyn and Tiago specifically, but was mostly just polite with the rest of them. Though she did like Rowan too—because everyone liked the man.

She simply murmured something noncommittal, then said, "I was just coming to find you. I can't thank you enough for what you did. If you hadn't been there..." Shaking her head, she let out a frustrated sigh.

"Where is Magnolia?"

The detective gave him a look he wasn't sure he could define, maybe surprise that he'd called Magnolia by her first name. "She and her son left." She blinked now as she stared hard at Ezra.

"Is that safe?"

"They're being escorted home by one of our officers and she's taking all necessary precautions. I was coming downstairs to let you know that you're free to go and thank you for your statement. If I have any follow-up questions, I'll reach out. I've got your number." She was still giving him a strange look.

He wanted to argue, but what was he going to say? Nothing at this point. And she wasn't the person he wanted to talk to anyway. Nope, that was Magnolia.

He slid his Bluetooth in as he headed out of the building, ignoring Adalyn as she called out to him. As he stepped out into the sunlight, he slid on his sunglasses and called Berlin, the newest addition to their misfit crew. None of them were ever going to fit into regular nine-to-five jobs or even normal professions.

"Heya," she said, her standard greeting.

"I need you to run someone's information for me. And it's personal. I want everything you have on her. *Everything*." Was he violating Magnolia's privacy? Yep. But if she'd had their son, he didn't care. And screw it, he wanted to know everything about her anyway, always had.

For years he'd managed to compartmentalize his past, to lock up memories of their time together. The best damn year of his life. In his dreams was the only time he hadn't been able to run from his past.

He was done running and was going to get some damn answers.

***

"I printed everything off for you since you're ancient." Berlin slid over the little packet she'd created, a smug grin on her face before she stood, strode to the bank of windows that overlooked the Central Business District. They had a special tint on them so no one could see in—and their windows were bullet-resistant.

Ezra didn't respond to the ancient comment because right about now he *felt* ancient. Instead, he hunched over the information on the conference room table and started reading.

"I'm just playing, man," Berlin murmured after a moment.

"I know. I'm...processing a lot right now." It was just the two of them at the office with the others back at the Victorian house in the Irish Channel district they used as a safe house of sorts.

This office was where everything was officially set up for taxes and all sorts of boring bullshit he didn't bother himself with. Their place of business fit in on the exterior anyway. Inside was a different story.

"I'm sorry," she murmured. "I wasn't trying to be insensitive. Of course you are if you just found out you had a kid."

"I'm not the father of her son." But as he looked through the paperwork, he realized maybe he was wrong.

"You sure about that?" Berlin's tone was neutral enough.

He glanced up but she wasn't even looking at him, just staring out the window at all the people below.

Refocusing, he zeroed in on at the date the kid had been born. Almost a Christmas baby. Then he did the math, sucked in a sharp breath. "I'm not sure of anything," he muttered more to himself than to the younger woman who was a terrifying genius.

They were lucky she'd come on board with them and wanted to help people. Because if she chose, Berlin could burn down the world. She was smart in the same way that Gage and Hailey were. He was just glad she was on their side.

"What about her husband?" he asked, when he finished looking through everything. Or scanning mostly, because it was a lot of content. He probably should have been more specific. "Henri Fontenot," he added when Berlin just frowned at him.

"She's never been married."

"No, she was. To a man named Henri Fontenot. I have no doubt."

Berlin cocked a dark eyebrow at him, but sat down in front of the laptop she carried with her everywhere. "If she kept your kid from you, it's seriously messed up, but objectively speaking, she's an impressive woman. She owns three boutique hotels and works with two women's shelters in the city and provides jobs to women transitioning out of abusive situations. And not shitty minimum wage jobs either. Really good stuff where they receive training for the future and are given retirement options. Not to mention the hotels they're working at offer childcare options twenty-four seven for their staff. That's incredibly rare. If she can't find the right work option in one of her hotels, she still tries to find them work. She's received so many awards in the last five years it's ridiculous."

Ezra couldn't even pretend to be surprised. She'd been talking about all the changes she wanted to make within her dad's companies even when she'd been seventeen. She'd had big plans even then. "Which is why it makes no sense that anyone wants to hurt her." How could anyone want to hurt Magnolia?

Berlin snorted. "It could literally be any number of abusive exes of the women she's helped over the years."

Right. He hadn't been thinking in broad terms, which wasn't like him. But he wasn't thinking clearly at all right now. Just consumed with the fact that Magnolia had a kid who might be his—probably was his—and that someone wanted to hurt her.

"Okay, Henri Fontenot. Oh woooow, he's stupid handsome." She let out a low whistle. "He's got that whole old money thing going on too. Comes from a wealthy family—"

"Enough." Ezra so didn't want to hear about some asshole who was the exact opposite of him.

"Aaaand he's also gay. Happily married with two kids—twins—to his, oh my god, adorable husband who looks like a teddy bear. Oh, and it looks like Magnolia was in their wedding so they're definitely friends. But nope, they were never married."

"I received a wedding invitation."

"From her?"

He paused. It hadn't had a return address, or if it had, he didn't remember. He just remembered ripping open the letter, being surprised to get one at all, and having the invitation fall out.

He'd burned the thing, unable to read it more than twice. Or eighteen times. And he could still repeat every single word of it.

"I don't know."

Berlin just gave him a hard look. "I think you need to talk to this woman and clear the air."

Yeah, that sounded like a really good idea. "I'll get this stuff later, okay? Are you heading out or working for a bit?"

"I need to finish some stuff up, but I'll be locking up soon."

He nodded, knowing she'd be safe here by herself, considering the security they had. But still found himself saying, "Text once you leave so I know you're good."

"Okay, Da—" Her eyes widened and she cut herself off. She often called him and Tiago *dad* jokingly because they were a little overprotective of her safety. She was the youngest of all of them. "Sorry, jeez."

But he laughed. "It's fine, seriously. Don't forget to text." Now he had to face the woman who'd very likely had their son and hadn't told him about it.

Too many emotions punched through him, but anger was winning. He might not have grown up like her, but keeping his son from him was bullshit.

And not something he would have ever expected from Magnolia.

CHAPTER 5

Never argue with a librarian.

Adalyn glanced over from the stove as Berlin walked into the kitchen of the Irish Channel house—their most used safe house. Redemption Harbor Security used this house as a sort of transition or safe house if any of their clients needed it. They'd recently helped two women escape a cult and they were now on their way to safety and a new start in Oregon. No one was here other than her, however, and she hadn't expected any company. "Hey, didn't expect you here tonight."

Berlin shrugged, dumped her big bag on the kitchen table. "Just left the office and I don't have any food at home. And I don't feel like stopping anywhere and talking or making eye contact with other humans so I figured I'd see what was in the fridge here."

Adalyn snickered at Berlin's bluntness. She was still getting to know the other woman—who was younger than all of them by about a decade. "Rowan's working on something with Tiago tonight and I'm here for the same reason." He'd even taken their dog, Gumbo, so she was feeling a little salty that he'd puppy-napped her buddy. "There's a ton of leftovers, none of which have expired." She started pulling out the boxes of mostly Italian food. "We really are animals." One of them needed to learn how to cook.

"Any Thai in there?"

"Ah...yes, one box and I'm pretty sure this is from Tuesday so it should be good."

Berlin grabbed glasses for both of them as she said, "Ezra's going to see his ex tonight."

"I can't believe he has a son. Or likely does. You should've seen the kid. Looks just like him." Adalyn plated food for both of them and put Berlin's in the microwave first.

"Pretty sure she's going to be one of our clients whether she wants it or not. Ezra had that determined look." Berlin slightly shook her head, her dark hair shot through with rainbow highlights swishing slightly against her shoulders.

Adalyn was pretty sure they were extensions but couldn't tell because they blended so perfectly. "Oh yeah. Rowan told me that he only mentioned Magnolia twice during the whole time they were stationed together, and both times he was drunk. Not that I'm trying to gossip! I'm just...worried about him." And she was. He'd looked almost shell-shocked back at the police station.

"No, I get it." Berlin glanced down at her cell phone at an incoming ping. She blinked in surprise. "Uh...we've got company."

"Here?" Adalyn blinked in surprise. They didn't advertise this place and only brought people here once they'd been vetted as real clients. It wasn't as if the place was a secret though; their neighbors thought it was a rental. Maybe it was a neighbor or solicitor.

Berlin turned her cell phone around and Adalyn looked at the cameras on-screen that showed the doorbell feed to the front door.

Antonia Collins stood on the front porch and, yep, there went the doorbell.

"What is she doing here?" she demanded. Antonia was the widow of the deceased Detective Rory Collins, one of Adalyn's childhood best friends. He'd been murdered earlier in the year, right during the Mardi Gras season, because of a case Adalyn had been working on. And the guilt still lived inside her, oppressive and heavy. She never should have asked him for help.

"I have as much information as you." Berlin's tone was dry. "Go grab the door and I'll heat up your food."

Adalyn just stood there, contemplating what to do. She could just...not answer the door. *Hmm.*

"You can't just leave her standing there."

"How the hell did she find this place?" Because Adalyn was certain the woman hadn't followed her. She'd been in the CIA for years and knew how to spot a tail.

"Again, I have as much information as you."

The doorbell sounded again.

"Damn it!" Steeling herself to talk to the woman who'd clearly hunted her down, she headed to the front door, pulled it open to find the petite Antonia Collins with her fist raised as if she was about to start pounding on the door.

The woman with dark hair, dark eyes and a lot of curves blinked up at Adalyn, then shoved a brown paper bag in Adalyn's face, shook it once. "I know you've been leaving money in my mailbox."

Ah, crap. Busted.

"Want to come in?" Adalyn stepped back even as she asked because this wasn't a conversation for their neighbors to see. Luckily their yard was huge and they had space from their neighbors, but still.

The woman couldn't be more than five feet two inches, but she had a big presence as she stalked inside, bag still in hand. Her T-shirt said *Librarian: keeper of books, giver of answers, guardian of knowledge.* And her expression said *I will destroy you if you piss me off.*

"How'd you find me?"

"I'm a librarian." Antonia sniffed imperiously.

"That still doesn't answer my question."

"I asked Fleur where to find you. I didn't even have to bribe her. She gave you up immediately." And she looked a little smug about that.

Adalyn bit back a grin at the woman's feistiness even as a bit of panic flooded her veins. Of course her sister had given her up.

"So you want to tell me what this is about?" Antonia held up the bag of cash again, waved it around.

Berlin chose that moment to poke her head out of the entryway to the kitchen down the hallway. "We've got food if you're hungry."

Adalyn sighed. *No, no, no.* This was not happening. They weren't inviting Antonia in for food. She needed to get her the hell out of here and convince her to just take the money and not ask questions.

Antonia looked up at her and maybe she read her expression because her grin was practically feral. "Sounds great." Then she shoved the bag at Adalyn again, forcing her to take it before she stomped down to the kitchen, her sneakers lighting up purple with each step.

Adalyn stepped into the kitchen, trying to regain control of the situation. "Look, this is just a misunderstanding—"

Antonia dropped her purse next to Berlin's bag and turned to face Adalyn, hands on hips as she stood next to the antique kitchen table. "So you haven't been leaving envelopes of cash in my mailbox?"

Berlin's mouth dropped open, but she quickly turned away and stuck her head in the refrigerator—as if that would make her invisible.

Adalyn cleared her throat. "Well—"

"No, you have been. The question was rhetorical! So what the hell is going on? Why have you been leaving me money? I know Rory wasn't involved in anything bad so if you try to tell me—"

"No, no, of course he wasn't. I feel guilty," she blurted. "And you weren't supposed to know."

"What the hell do you feel guilty about? Because I know he wasn't cheating on me."

Adalyn blinked again. "No, he never would have," she murmured. Rory Collins had loved his wife to distraction. His girls too. "Can we sit?" She motioned to the table, needing to sit for this conversation.

The woman yanked out a chair so Adalyn sat across from her, was surprised when Berlin set a bottle of opened white wine between them along with two glasses.

Adalyn nodded at Berlin when she held up the bottle because why the hell not? She rarely drank but tonight called for it. She cleared her throat again, trying to find the right words. "It's my fault Rory was killed." *Murdered.* But she hated saying the word, let alone thinking it. Hated everything that had gone down. "If I'd never called him about the man hunting me, then he'd have been on his way to see you and your girls. He'd have never gotten caught in the crossfire by that sick bastard." She couldn't give Antonia all the details—even the police and Feds didn't know everything—but she could admit this much.

Antonia blinked, the tightness in her shoulders easing slightly as she leaned back in her chair. "*That's* why you've been leaving me money? I *know* you reached out to Rory. He told me he was helping you with something before...before everything went to hell. But I don't blame you." And she sounded confused that Adalyn blamed herself.

"It's my fault—"

"Oh my god." Antonia shook her head. "He was killed by a psychopath who wanted to hurt a whole lot of people. Unfortunately my husband was one of them. And the reality is that he could have been killed in a car accident or in a boating accident or from a heart attack or any number of things. Am I heartbroken? Absolutely. I don't know that I'll ever recover. And if I didn't have my girls, I'd probably be a bigger mess than I am. But you're not taking on the guilt of his death. That's madness. Because I know you tried to save him that night. I've seen the videos. You're not at fault. And while I appreciate the gesture, it's misguided. He had a large life insurance policy and we're doing okay." She stood, her wine still untouched.

Adalyn stood with her. "Will you keep it for the girls, then? For their college or whatever they decide to do? Maybe if I set up scholarships for them so it's all on the up and up? Or just put money into their accounts if they have them?" Because yeah, leaving envelopes of cash in the woman's mailbox was pretty weird. Adalyn had been swimming in guilt all year though, and trying to alleviate it somehow.

"That...is actually okay. We've got college savings accounts for all of them. I can send you a link to add money to them if you feel like it." Antonia gave her a small smile now. "And I probably shouldn't have barged over here but it's been a long day."

"No, you had every right to. But how'd you know it was me leaving the money?" Because Adalyn had been careful to avoid her cameras and Antonia's neighbor's cameras, choosing to put the money in her mailbox instead of on the front porch.

Antonia shrugged. "Installed new cameras in the front yard in one of the trees. You were always pretty good about wearing hoodies and it was always at night but I got the high-tech kind. I paid for it with some of the money you left."

Adalyn let out a little laugh. She really did like this woman. "I promise no more weird envelopes of cash from me. And I'm sorry—"

"No more apologies. I'm just sorry we didn't get to know each other be-fore...everything."

"Yeah, me too." Even more than she'd realized now that she was standing in front of Rory's widow.

"Glad to hear that because you're coming over to dinner on Sunday. We eat at six. We're having tacos." She picked up her purse. "You can tell the girls stories about their dad from high school."

Adalyn started to protest.

But Berlin piped in. "She'll be there." Berlin was sitting at the island top, shoveling food into her mouth while on her phone. She didn't even look up as she answered for Adalyn.

She swallowed back her original words and nodded. "I'll be there."

"Good." Nodding once at Berlin, Antonia left a lot more quietly than she'd arrived.

"I could have had plans on Sunday," Adalyn grumbled as she went to reheat her food.

Berlin simply snorted her thoughts on that. Then she said, "You should bring Gumbo with you. You'll be a hit with the kids."

"That's really smart." Dogs were always a great distraction, especially one as cute as Gumbo.

"Don't sound so surprised. I'm a certified evil genius." Her grin was mischievous as she stood up, took her plate to the sink. "I'm gonna game for a bit. Want to join me? We can do two-player mode."

"Nah. But I'll hang out here with you." It was the first night she'd had off in a while so maybe she'd catch up on reading.

Or *maaaaybe* she'd reach out to the others and find out if they knew what was going on with Ezra and his long-lost ex. Some habits really died hard. After being in the CIA for so long, she liked knowing everything about everyone. Some people called that being nosy, but she just liked being informed.

CHAPTER 6

Ezra cruised down the quiet cobblestone road, pressed answer on his motorcycle helmet's Bluetooth when Hailey's name popped up. The tech had come a long way in the last twenty years—and he had a hell of a lot nicer bike than he had when he'd been younger too. "Hey short stuff."

"Hey yourself," she said. "I hear things are getting a little wild down there. You want me to come visit? Jesse always likes an excuse to look at real estate."

He laughed lightly as he pulled up behind a sleek white BMW idling at the four-way stop. "I'm good, promise. I know you guys are busy anyway. What job are you working on now?" he asked, mainly because he didn't want to talk about his personal life. As a rule, he never wanted to talk about his past, but Hailey was one of the few people who knew about Magnolia. As little as he'd told her anyway.

"I know you're changing the subject, but fine. We just brought down a big group of assholes trafficking people through a port in Jacksonville. I'm glad to be home, but even happier that we were able to help."

He was sure there was more to the story, and wanted to hear it, but his head was too messed up right now. "Good." He paused as he turned onto Magnolia's street, tension bunching inside him. "I don't know what the hell to say to her," he blurted. "I need advice how to handle this." Something he rarely if ever had said to anyone. But it was easier to talk to Hailey since he wasn't looking at her right now—and he trusted her. Of all his friends, he didn't think there was a judgmental bone in her body.

Hailey's answer was immediate. "*Ask* for the truth. Find out what happened and why she kept this from you if he's your son. And...I looked at the information Berlin compiled. It's thorough. I did a little dive on the woman because I couldn't help myself and didn't find anything new. On the surface and from your own experiences, she's not a bad person. So when you go into this, don't be accusatory. Just talk to her and keep a level voice and head. Because at the end of the day, if that kid is yours and you go in there acting like a douche, you'll ruin things before they start. That's his mom, the woman who raised him."

He shoved out a breath as he pulled into a spot a few houses down from her place. There was a large, stately fence lining her property, complete with a security gate. But he wasn't sure if she'd buzz him in so he decided to park here and hope for the best. "I don't think I could yell at her anyway." He was beyond pissed, but at the end of the day...this was Magnolia. And Hailey was right. "I'll assume the best and expect the worst."

"There you go. One of the mottos I live by. Always expect the worst."

He snort-laughed as he shut his bike off. "No doubt. All right, I'm parked. I'll talk to you later." Because he needed to do this now before he changed his mind.

Once they disconnected, all that tension was back, bunching in his shoulders and down his spine. And now a heavy rock had settled in his gut to even things out. Especially because he wasn't sure if she'd reject him. He hadn't called her, even though he'd known it was a risk just showing up like this.

The sun was down, but the neighborhood had plenty of streetlights and most of the yards, walls or fences had different solar lights illuminating everything, including the addition of Christmas and Hannukah decorations.

At Magnolia's gate, he buzzed the little keypad and made sure his face was clear in the camera. He was surprised when the gate opened a few seconds later. Then her voice came over the intercom. "Just come on up to the front door. If you drove, feel free to park in the driveway."

So surprised by her immediately letting him in, Ezra didn't even trust his voice and simply strode through the opening gate instead of going back to get his ride.

Because not so deep down, he was worried that she'd change her mind and reject him entrance.

And if that wasn't a metaphor for how he'd felt their entire relationship... "Jesus, get it together," he growled to himself as he stalked down the driveway. Light-up candy canes illuminated the entire drive.

It wasn't too long, just a simple driveway that led to the garage of the stately two-story brick house with lush foliage, even this late in the year. The place looked like her too. Warm, welcoming, elegant and beautiful. A giant Christmas tree was visible through one of the windows, golds and reds sparkling.

As he reached the front steps, the door swung open and there she was.

Magnolia Lavigne. The girl, now woman, of his dreams. Still. Because nothing had changed in that respect.

He had one type. Her.

And he hated that.

Her dark hair was pulled up in a sort of bun thing on her head, loose with a few strands falling out and framing her face. In dark jeans and a soft-looking cream-colored sweater, and socks covered in reindeer—he imagined this was what she normally looked like when relaxing at home.

Though nothing about her expression was relaxed.

"You can come in if you want." She stepped back, motioning for him to come inside.

And he hated the way his heart kicked against his chest, beating overtime just because he was in her vicinity. Simply nodding, he shoved his hands in his pockets and stepped inside, the subtle scents of cinnamon and vanilla lifting in the air.

"Is he mine?" he blurted. "The kid?"

Magnolia gave him a strange look, then softly snorted. "Uh, *yeah*." Then she sighed and motioned for him to follow. "Come on, let's sit in the kitchen. Lucas isn't here so we can talk freely."

He wasn't sure about that look, or that tone. As if he should already know that the kid—Lucas—was his. As he followed after, he got an entire snapshot of their lives in a wall of pictures.

His throat tightened as he saw them one by one, Magnolia and Lucas on his first day of kindergarten, on a vacation somewhere sunny and warm, the two of them making silly faces at the camera with snorkeling masks on. Later ones when he was probably twelve, the two of them dressed up and standing outside the Saenger Theater, probably for a play. Pictures with Lucas and his grandparents, Lucas and random people he didn't know. Probably Magnolia's relatives or friends. Lucas standing in front of an older-looking Jeep, his arm wrapped around his mom's shoulders and smiling widely as he held up the keys.

Blood rushed in his ears, wild and loud, but somehow he managed to get himself under control, to breathe, as he stepped into the sparkling kitchen with high ceilings. There were more pictures in here, but all over the refrigerator. So he didn't look at them.

"I kind of want to ask how you found out where I live, but I guess it's not too hard," she murmured as she pulled out a bottle of water from the fridge, set it in front of him.

"A friend of mine looked you up. You've done a lot for the city, just like you always wanted," he murmured as he sat at the island top. There was a bowl of fruit and a bowl of nuts and other healthy snacks.

She pulled out a little cheese tray, some type of muffins that looked fresh, then a bag of crackers and set them in front of him. "The crackers go good with the cheese. And the muffins are zucchini but they're good. Eat," she murmured and he wondered if it was an old habit that had never died, or just her way. Because she'd always been feeding him, trying to take care of him when they'd been together. Clearing her throat, she continued, "I know you're not here to talk about me so let's just get down to it."

Well, that wasn't necessarily true, but he nodded all the same. "Okay, so why didn't you tell me about him?" Did his voice sound steady? He couldn't tell, because blood was still rushing in his ears like a freight train.

She blinked at him, then let out a harsh, angry laugh. "Are you really going to play it that way?"

"I don't know what you're talking about."

She stared at him hard for a long moment. Then she said, "I called you so many times, texted you too. But your phone was disconnected. I *tried* to tell you about him. So many times."

When he went to interrupt, she held up a hand.

"I'm not done. I went to your house, the one you lived in on Wilson Circle. You were gone, and so was your dad. I guess the owner kicked your dad out because there was a For Sale sign. I talked to the woman who lived next door. I either don't remember her name or never learned it, but she was chain smoking the entire time we talked and said you used to mow her lawn sometimes. She called you a good boy. She also told me that you'd left, had signed up for the Marines and were heading to Camp Pendleton."

Ezra nodded, stunned. Mrs. Dantzler had indeed been his chain-smoking neighbor. She'd had a hard life, but had always had a kind word for him, had occasionally let him crash in her living room when his dad had gone on a bender. "Yeah, I signed up after you ended things with me, told me never to contact you again."

She blinked, real surprise in her pretty blue eyes. "I *never* ended things with you. You ghosted me! You just disappeared, as if..." Her voice cracked on the last word. "As if nothing between us mattered. But I *still* sent letters, trying to let you know about Lucas. It took a while but I managed to find an address. Lucas had been born by then. I included pictures and—" She turned away from him, her voice cracking again as she gave him her back.

He was moving before he could stop himself, before he was even fully aware, and rounded the island, desperate to touch her, to...comfort her. "I never received any letters," he managed to rasp out. Because none of this was what he'd expected. He reached out a hand to touch her shoulder, but let it drop. He didn't have the right to touch her anymore, hadn't for a long time. "I received your wedding invitation."

She swiveled then, tears tracking down her cheeks, but she angrily dashed them away. "What the hell are you talking about?" She took a little step back from him and he realized he was towering over her.

So he stepped back, sat at the island again. He'd used his size against people to get what he wanted, namely assholes who deserved it. But never with women, and never, ever with Magnolia. "Yep. I received a wedding invitation that I now know—as in only an hour ago—wasn't real. It was for you and a man name Henri Fontenot."

She blinked. "Henri?" Then she snorted out a brittle laugh. "Definitely not real."

"I know I've said it, but I never ghosted you."

"And I never ended things with you." She stared at him for a loooong, hard moment. "And I believe that you're telling the truth." She sounded shocked by that. "Oh my god, you never *knew* about Lucas?"

"No. And I didn't ghost you," he said again, because screw that. He wanted that crystal clear between them. As if he could have *ever* walked away from her.

He couldn't read her expression at all; her pretty blue eyes were mostly just shocked. Then she frowned, looked down at her phone, winced. Then groaned. "Mari is here. Can you just stay put?" She didn't wait for his answer as she left, her movements jerky as she rushed from the kitchen.

What the hell had just happened?

CHAPTER 7

When life gives you lemons, add vodka.

Magnolia stepped back as her best friend barreled into the foyer in dark jeans, a snug red sweater and four-inch heels the same bright red, with a little bow by the toes. She was pretty sure they were Valentino. "You look gorgeous. Why so dressed up? Meetings today?"

Mari, a pilot who now owned three private airports, normally wore jeans, sneakers and a pullover. Or shorts and T-shirts in summer. But when she dressed up, it either meant she had a date or meetings that she loathed. "No way, we're not talking about me. But thank you, I love these heels—what happened? Are you okay?" She eyed Magnolia as if looking for damage.

"I'm okay...ish. Today has been long. And weird. Ezra's here," she blurted because ten seconds was the longest she could hold out telling her best friend. A woman who was her sister in all the ways that mattered.

Mari's mouth fell open. "Wait, here, *here*? As in your house?" Her hands balled into fists and the sight made Magnolia want to laugh.

And cry.

And hug her.

She stepped in front of Mari. "Yes and you're not going to do whatever it is you're thinking right now. Besides, I need a hug."

Mari didn't pause, just launched herself at her and wrapped her arms around her tightly. "I'll make sure no one ever finds the body," she whisper-growled as she bear-hugged her.

Despite the craptastic day she'd had, she laughed, and oh god, it felt good. "I believe you. And listen, I don't think he ghosted me," she said as Mari stepped back. "I think he was just as in the dark as I was about some things." Magnolia held up a hand when Mari went to argue. "I promise I'll tell you everything, but I need to talk with him."

Mari's cheeks flushed hot, but she finally said. "Fine. But first, where's Lucas? Is my sweet boy okay?" Ever the fierce aunt who would do anything to protect him.

"He's at the MacElroys' so I know he's safe." Just down the street, only four houses away. "And before you ask, I don't know who shot at me."

"Yeah you do."

"Well, I don't know for sure," she muttered. "How'd you even know about what happened?"

"Camila texted me."

Magnolia couldn't even get mad. She sighed. "You're staying the night, aren't you?" She flicked a glance down at the leather weekender bag Mari had owned since they were eighteen.

"Uh yeah. I'm not leaving you." She held her palms up. "I'll go make myself at home in the guest suite. But if you change your mind." She pounded one fist into her open palm. "I will destroy everything that he is and everything he cares about."

"You sound like a crazy villain when you say stuff like that."

"Doesn't make it any less true." She plucked up her bag, set the strap on her shoulder. "Come get me once he's gone."

"I will. And thank you for being you."

Mari just grinned and headed toward the stairs.

Steeling herself, she headed back into the kitchen, found Ezra sitting at her island top looking more gorgeous than any man had a right to. Jesus, he just got better with age. He was eating some of the cheese, and some primal instinct had her gaze flicking down to his hands.

His big, callused, very talented hands. It didn't matter how many years had passed between them, she remembered everything he'd done with those wicked, wonderful hands.

Aaaand now was so not the time to even think about that. Not now. Not ever. She leaned against the countertop across from him and just watched him, trying to figure out what the hell to say.

"I..." Nope. That wouldn't work. She sighed. *Words! Come on brain, get it together.*

Thankfully, he gave her a lopsided smile and it was like the years between them vanished for this one small moment. "Today is weird."

She let out a startled laugh. "That's an understatement. I don't even know what to say right now. I was so mad at you for so long and then eventually I just boxed it all up." Reaaaalllly healthy, according to her therapist. She nearly snorted. "And now..." She rubbed her hands over her face, wishing she had a pillow to scream into.

"Who was shooting at you and why?"

His question brought her out of her head, made her focus on him. "I'm not totally sure."

"But you have an idea who." There was a dark glint in his eyes, one that sent a shiver down her spine.

This was the Ezra she remembered, the one with the dangerous edge she'd fallen hard and fast for. "I do."

"Who?" A single question, his voice hard.

"It doesn't matter."

"It very much matters. I work in security. Let me help you with this problem. Because I'm helping regardless. It'll just be easier if you give me all the information I need up front."

She blinked once. Again. "So are we just not talking about Lucas?"

"I figured you needed a break, and honestly I do too." He'd taken off his jacket, had hooked it on the chair behind him, and his long-sleeved T-shirt was shoved up, showing off gorgeous forearms. That she was totally not going to notice. Nope.

"And this is a problem I can help you with," he continued, oblivious to her practically drooling over his forearms. "Because that psycho took a shot at you in the middle of the day with people around. Who do you think it is?"

So he wasn't wrong about her not wanting to talk about their son. Mainly because it was simply too much to process right now, especially since she had a good idea who'd come between them. And she really, really didn't want to think about that. It hurt too much.

A little ache in her chest throbbed, and nope. *No, no, no.* She had to focus on the threat and just lock up everything else. For tonight only. Because tomorrow she was going to get her answers.

She pushed away from the countertop, paced a little because she needed to move. "I think it's a man named Samuel Perry. He's sent me threatening emails, has shown up at one of the hotels I manage and..." She shoved her hands in her pockets because they were starting to tremble. "He's a horrible man. He used to abuse his wife and she finally left him thanks to the encouragement of some friends. She stayed at a shelter I work with and the owner eventually put her in touch with me. I help abuse victims find jobs and transition into working again, getting financial independence."

She took a deep breath, not wanting to get into all of that now. Ezra was such a good listener that it was easy to open up to him.

"Anyway, he hunted her down to her new job and I happened to be there when he was threatening her. She tried to stand up to him, but I could see the fear in her eyes so I got in his face while waiting on security. Then I banned him from all the establishments my company runs. His ex also has a restraining order, but he's a violent angry man. The bans and order won't stop him. And he's gotten it into his head that I'm the reason, or at least part of the reason, his ex won't talk to him. He tried to shove me and I dodged him, swiped his legs out from under him, and kept her physically safe. It embarrassed him, and if security hadn't shown up when they did..." She trailed off, not wanting to relive that day.

She'd acted on instinct, using the training from her weekly self-defense classes. But she hadn't thought much past just stopping him from attacking. Sure, she'd managed to take him off guard, but she wasn't sure she could have held her own against him. He was big and strong and full of rage.

"What are the police doing to keep you safe?" There was a bite to his words, just as her phone buzzed again.

She bit back a curse as she looked at the incoming request from the front gate's security cameras. *Oh, nooooo.* It was her parents. Apparently she was going to have to deal with things sooner than later.

"I hate to do this, but do you mind waiting again? I need to handle this." And have a conversation she'd been hoping to put off until tomorrow morning. But it seemed like she didn't get to be a coward tonight after all.

Ezra nodded, but she could see the frustration on his face. His rugged, handsome face and gorgeous full lips.

She forced herself to look away, to make her legs move and guide her out of the kitchen.

"Baby." Her mom pulled her into a giant hug, her Chanel No. 5 subtly trailing her in a little cloud. "How are you? Where's Lucas? Why aren't there police here? Is Mari here? I saw her car outside."

Oh, this was going to be a lot. "I'm okay," she murmured as she stepped back, hugging her dad as well even as she prepared to ask them hard questions. "And Lucas is at a neighbor's house. He's fine. The police are handling things, but they certainly can't be here all the time. Mari's in one of the guest rooms working." She had no idea if Mari was, but Magnolia didn't need an audience for this regardless. She motioned for them to come into the living room. "We need to talk about something."

Her mother frowned, but her father simply headed into the living room, waiting for her mom to sit before he sat next to her on the little love seat angled by the main window. It competed for space with the giant Christmas tree she and Lucas had put up a few weeks ago.

Magnolia couldn't sit, not with so much energy pummeling through her, so she leaned next to the electric fireplace. For a moment, she thought about trying to be delicate, to soften her questions.

But no, she wanted the truth and would only get it if she surprised them. Something her dad had taught her long ago when they'd first gone into business together. *Sometimes you have to ambush people. It's the only way to get to the truth.*

"What did you hear about today? Because obviously someone told you what happened."

"Oh, Lucas texted me, told me that some lunatic tried to shoot you. I should have heard it from my daughter though." Her mom's tone was only slightly scolding. "But I can imagine how scary that was. At least you've got great security here."

Okay so they didn't seem to know about Ezra. That would help this whole ambush thing at least. "I do. Luckily someone saved me, tackled me out of the way from being shot."

"Thank god," her father murmured, shaking his head. "The world has gone mad, I swear. I think we should talk about getting you a driver, at least for now."

"Ezra Hunt saved me." She paused, watching their reactions. Her mom frowned in confusion. Her dad... oh, no. She saw the flash in his gaze. "He also had no idea about Lucas until just today. He thinks I broke up with him all those years ago, and never received any letters from me." She watched her dad as she spoke, because she knew his tells. "And I believe him. Dad, did you meddle in our relationship?"

"Oh darling, your father never would have done that..." Her mom trailed off as she glanced at her father, seeing the same thing Magnolia did. The truth. "Oh, Arnold. You didn't. Tell me you didn't." She breathed out the last few words in horror.

"That boy was no good—"

"No!" Rage swelled inside her and it took all her self-control not to shout, to let loose the way she truly wanted. "He was just from the wrong side of the tracks, according to you. But he was a good person. Why does he think I broke up with him?"

For a moment her father was silent, his jaw working as he ground his molars. Then he stood, stalked to the window overlooking the front yard full of Christmas cheer. "I sent him a text from your phone. You were in some school thing. A play I think. And I saw the texts between the two of you, the 'plans' you had to move in together after high school." His voice was a little mocking and oh, that pissed her off even more. "I ended things with him, then blocked his number. You guys didn't go to the same school and didn't run in the same circles. It was worth the risk." And he didn't even sound sorry.

She wanted to throw up.

"What about the letters I sent him telling him about Lucas?"

He swiveled. "I had nothing to do with that! Which just goes to show you he didn't care about Lucas at all. So I'd been right to interfere."

"You're wrong." Ezra strode into the room now, huge, intimidating and exactly like the man she'd known he would grow into. Powerful. His voice was just as quiet as Magnolia's, but there was no mistaking the underlying edge. "I never got any letters. I joined the Marines because Magnolia...because I thought she'd broken up with me. There was nothing left for me here without her."

She was definitely going to be sick.

"Get out," she snapped.

Ezra looked at her in shock.

"Not you." She went to reach for him, stopped herself, then turned to her father. "You. Out. Now. I can't look at you. And I don't want to say something I'll regret."

"Magnolia—"

"No." This from her mother, who'd already stood, picked up her purse. She looked furious as she glared at her father. "I'm so disappointed in you, Arnold. More than I ever thought possible." She turned to look at Magnolia, tears glittering in blue eyes that were a mirror to hers. "I'll call you tomorrow?"

Magnolia nodded and refused to look at her father as they left. Only once the front door shut behind them did she allow herself to crumple on the nearest couch. "Ezra, I'm so sorry. I had no idea." Nausea pushed up inside her even as tears pricked her eyes. "I should have tried harder—"

"No, you don't get to take on that guilt." He sat next to her, looking lost as he watched her. He scrubbed his hands over his face. "This was all your father. And it sounds like you did try. Jesus, so many years."

Ignoring his body language—because Ezra had always held himself apart—she leaned forward and pulled him into a hug.

To her surprise, he wrapped his arms around her tight. She buried her face against his neck and resisted the urge to crawl into his lap. But she needed to hold on to someone right now. No, not someone, just Ezra, who understood what she was going through, to an extent.

And it had to be worse for him—he'd lost so many years with his son. "I don't know if I'll ever forgive him for taking all those years from you," she whispered against his neck. "From Lucas."

He rubbed a hand down her back but didn't respond. Just held her in that way that shouldn't be familiar, but was nonetheless.

She tightened her grip for a moment, then made herself pull back. "Sorry," she muttered, wiping away the last of the tears. "I shouldn't be crying, not when you've lost..." She swallowed hard.

To her surprise, he cupped her jaw, rubbed a callused thumb over her cheek as he stared at her.

And just like that, she tumbled back almost seventeen years. Hell, eighteen, to the first time she'd met him. She'd been absolutely smitten, and she'd found out later that he had been as well. He'd just been able to mask his reaction to her a lot better.

Right now, he wasn't masking anything as his gaze fell on her mouth, hot and hungry, and yep, that familiar ache was back.

One she hadn't experienced in so very long it seemed as if it had been a dream. A different life. Heck, it *had* been a different life. She'd been a different person, full of dreams and a vision of how her life would look.

"Ezra," she whispered, no idea what she wanted to say.

He let out a moan, so low she wasn't sure if she'd imagined it, but then he leaned slightly forward.

And the front door banged open.

She jumped back, blinking away the haze of lust as she turned toward the foyer to see Lucas striding in, his backpack on his shoulders. "Mari's car is in the driveway so I couldn't get to the garage..." He trailed off from calling out to her as he usually did when he realized she was in the living room. With someone else. "Oh. Hi." He gave his mom a confused look, but then smiled politely at Ezra. "You're the guy from the police station. Is everything okay?"

"Oh yes." Nervous, she stood up and rounded the couch. "We're just talking about something. I made snacks in the kitchen and Mari's in one of the guest rooms if you want to go see her."

Lucas nodded, clearly understanding she wanted privacy, then dropped a kiss on her cheek before heading down the hallway to the kitchen. Likely to eat half the food in the fridge. She missed having that metabolism.

Aaand none of that mattered now. She turned back to Ezra, who'd already stood and was looking unreadable. And a little uncomfortable.

"I'm sorry, I haven't told him about you yet. I'd planned to, but then he wanted to know about the shooting and the threats I've been receiving. And by the time we got back here...I chickened out," she whispered.

Ezra shoved his hands in his pockets. "It's okay. And if you don't want to tell him, it's okay—"

"Are you serious right now?" She stared up at him, wishing she had heels on so there wasn't so much of a height difference.

"I don't know." He ran a hand over dark hair he still wore a little long. "I don't know anything right now. I just don't want you to feel pressured or—"

"Okay, we're going to stop that right now."

He blinked.

"What?" she demanded.

"I forgot how bossy you are. Always surprising coming from such a small package."

She snickered despite the tension coiled inside her. "I'm not bossy. I'm just always right. And we'll set up a time to introduce you," she said, lowering her voice. "I'll talk to him tonight, tell him everything. God, he's...well I don't know how he'll react. But oh, wait, I need your number. And you need mine. Though since you found my house I'm guessing you won't have trouble with my cell."

He just gave her a small grin.

Ooooh she felt that one all the way to her core. So she ignored the feeling and pulled her cell out of her pocket. Not trusting her trembling fingers—and not wanting him to see how affected she was—she opened her phone and held it out to him. "Just put your number in. I'll call you in the morning and let you know how things went."

He took her phone, his fingers brushing hers as he did. And she didn't think it was her imagination that he felt that spark too.

"You can call or text me anytime. You don't have to wait until tomorrow." His deep voice wrapped around her, made her feel lightheaded.

She had to actively order herself not to step closer to him, to not hug him.

He cleared his throat. "If you want to smooth over what your dad did when you tell him...it's okay. Well, it's not okay, but I'll understand. He's his grandfather."

She stared up at him, floored by his words. "My father never understood you," she murmured, then shook her head slightly. "And no. I'll tell him everything. He deserves the truth. My dad made some really bad choices and he'll have to live with them. Not you."

He paused, but then nodded and let himself out.

And it was like he took all the heat with him. Sighing, she locked the door and headed to the kitchen. She had to do this now. Not because she thought she'd lose her nerve, but Ezra deserved for her to tell Lucas as soon as possible.

She'd worry about what happened after this later. As soon as he left, she armed her security system and then double-checked that all her security cameras were on as well.

She could only deal with so much stress and she needed to know that her family, including Mari, was safe in her house.

CHAPTER 8

"Thanks, I owe you," Ezra said into his cell.

"Nah, we're good." Scarlett, a former detective now turned private security, said. "Besides, I know her name. Well, her reputation. I'll pull in someone with me for tonight so we're watching her house at different angles. We'll keep her place locked down."

"Thank you. Also...if she or her son leave, keep someone on each of them." Ezra would tell Magnolia about the security he was temporarily hiring, but for tonight he needed to know she was safe. He was tempted to simply sit on her house himself, but figured that bringing in two women for security would go over better for any local police doing a drive-by of her neighborhood. Especially since Scarlett had a good relationship with the department.

"Absolutely. How long do you want me to watch them?"

"Tonight and tomorrow at least. I'm going to talk to her tomorrow but she was overwhelmed tonight." He was too, if he was being honest.

"Sounds good. I've got my phone on me. I'll text or call with any issues."

"Thanks." As he disconnected, he pulled onto the quiet street of the company's safe house. The new branch of Redemption Harbor Security in New Orleans had recently bought a big house they used as a place for people to lie low, to transition, or to plain hide out.

And he'd decided to come here tonight instead of going home.

Because his condo was depressing. Oh it was nice, expensive and had all the luxuries he'd never even imagined as a kid. But it had never been home. And being inside Magnolia's place, filled with so much love and personality, only hit even harder how much he was just existing.

He had good friends, had done a lot of stuff he was proud of. But something had been missing for a long time. And he knew what it was.

Inside the house he wasn't surprised to find Berlin gaming in the living room, a VR headset over her face as she kicked and punched at the air, yelling excitedly at the random people she gamed with online.

Adalyn was sitting in the cushy chair by the fireplace, a book in hand. She smiled when she saw him. "Hey. Didn't expect you here tonight."

"Didn't feel like going home."

"I feel that. Neither Gumbo or my man are at home." Adalyn stood, stretched. "You hungry? There's a ton in the fridge."

"I'm good. So...I went by her place."

Adalyn froze, blinked.

"Hold on guys, I'll be back," Berlin said, then ripped her headset off, set it next to a lamp on one of the side tables before sitting on the ground and stretching her legs out. Her sweaty hair was plastered to her face, her eyes wide. "So what happened?"

Adalyn sat back down as well, nodded. "Yeah, tell us everything."

It was a hell of a lot easier to open up to them than the guys and he wasn't sure why. But he laid everything out, right down to when Magnolia had ordered her father to leave. At first he'd thought she was kicking *him* out, but when he'd realized she was telling her father to leave... He'd already believed she'd been telling the truth, but that had taken care of any doubts that might have crept in later.

"I also got security for her and her son, for at least tonight and tomorrow. And I want to do a deep dive on Samuel Perry." He'd filled them in on the asshole who'd shot at her as well. Or allegedly. "I know the cops are trying to find him, but you're better," he said to Berlin.

"Compliments will get you everywhere." She grinned slightly, but nodded. "I'll find the guy and we'll nail him to the wall."

"So...what's your son like?" Adalyn asked.

"I don't know." He shrugged, the action not as smooth as he was going for. "She said she was going to tell him everything tonight." And Ezra kept worrying that Lucas wouldn't care about meeting him. Wouldn't want to. That was the worst-case scenario, the one that kept playing in his head.

"Stop," Adalyn murmured, leaning back in her chair. "The kid is gonna want to meet you."

"I didn't say anything."

Adalyn simply shrugged.

"Fine. I'm nervous."

"That's normal."

"Yeah." Berlin nodded in agreement. "But it's going to work out."

He didn't have her optimism, but managed a small smile anyway. Sort of. When his phone buzzed, his heart kicked against his chest to see Magnolia's name. It had been so damn long since her name had popped up on his screen.

I told him everything. Mari sat with us and confirmed what happened back then. He's upset at his grandfather, but wants to meet you. So the ball is in your court. Also...a detective buzzed my gate, said that a private security company is keeping an eye on my house. Do you know anything about that?

Busted. *I called in a favor, asked a couple people to watch your place. You need extra security right now and they're pros. And I'm ready to meet him anytime, anywhere.*

Little dots appeared, then disappeared, then appeared again.

"Wow," Adalyn murmured.

He looked up as he waited. "What?"

"Nothing. Just...never seen that expression on your face before."

He frowned. "What expression?"

But she simply shrugged.

And Berlin rolled up from the floor. "I'm going to start digging into that asshole. I'll let you know what I find."

Nodding, he sat back on the couch even though he wanted to pace. Or go a few rounds with a punching bag. Energy sliced through him in sharp waves, the anticipation and fear of meeting the son he'd never known about. And yeah, of seeing Magnolia again.

But she wasn't asking for any sort of relationship or anything. They might have had a moment back at her house, but he wasn't stupid. She'd built a nice life for herself, and while she was letting him in, he knew it was only so far.

His phone buzzed again, another incoming text. And yep, his heart rate kicked up in response.

Thank you for the security. I want to say it's unnecessary, but even with our security and cameras, I'm grateful. More little dots popped up, then another message came through. *Lucas took things so well. I mean, well enough. He's really mad at my dad, but he's so steady about this.*

"I'm gonna head up," Adalyn murmured. "You staying the night?"

"Ah, yeah. Should I set the alarm? Or is Rowan coming by later?"

"He and Tiago are working on something so just set it. He knows the code if he decides to come over."

He nodded and texted back. *Kids are resilient.* Or at least that was what he'd heard. *What did you tell him about me? Before, I mean.* Even as he texted the question, regret filled him. He wasn't sure he wanted the answer.

He only asked once and I was as honest as I could be. I told him I didn't know where you were, but that you were serving your country.

He shouldn't be surprised that she hadn't thrown him under the bus. Considering what she'd assumed about him, he'd have understood if she'd told him that Ezra had abandoned them. But no, she wouldn't have said that anyway. That simply wasn't her.

I know I don't need to thank you, but thank you for letting me into his life. Texting made things a lot easier, to say the words he normally wouldn't have been able to get out.

You definitely don't have to thank me for that. And if we're being thankful, thank you for saving my life today. I don't know if I ever said that. Everything is still blurry.

You don't have to thank me for that either.

She sent him a smiling emoji. Then... *So, when do you want to officially meet him? Is tomorrow morning okay? You can come over here for breakfast.*

That sounds good, he responded immediately even as all his stomach muscles tightened. Good, terrifying, same thing.

We'll see you at eight. Then she included another emoji, this one with little hearts.

Aaand he didn't know how to respond. No way was he going to turn into someone who dissected texts. But still, he sent back a smiling emoji nonetheless. The first emoji he'd ever sent.

And he was lying to himself because he was going to think about those heart emojis all night.

CHapTer 9

Ezra stepped into the side door of the kitchen after a five-mile run, not surprised to find Rowan here. He grinned as the scent of the dark roast filled the air. "You made coffee." Good thing too because he hadn't slept much last night.

"Always. Didn't even realize you were out running."

"Yeah, couldn't sleep. How's that thing you and Tiago are working on that no one is allowed to know about? Except Gumbo, apparently."

Rowan grinned, shrugged, leaned against the countertop and took a sip of his coffee with a happy sigh. As if she heard her name, Gumbo came running in, her little tail wagging happily.

She greeted Rowan first, then came to sit in front of Ezra, waiting for pets. So he obliged, because how could he not? The mutt was a cute ball of fluff and energy.

"I'm going to make breakfast before Adalyn and I head home, but I hear you've got breakfast plans already."

"Ah, yeah." He poured his coffee, the only thing he could handle now anyway. "Not sure what I'm going to say but..." Lifting a shoulder, he covered his expression with his mug. Because he had no clue about anything right now.

"I'm happy for you. I mean, not about what happened, but I'm glad that you know about your son now. And maybe you and Magnolia—"

"No. I know what you're going to say, but no. It's been a long time and she's clearly built a good life for her and her...our son."

"It's not like there's limited room in her life for people."

Ezra cleared his throat, then crouched down and gave Gumbo more pets. Petting the dog was easier than this conversation. "I don't know if I should bring anything."

"Nah, just your sunny disposition." There was a hint of humor in Rowan's voice.

He eyed his friend as he stood back up. "Ha, ha. She looked good," he murmured, unable to stop the words from pouring out.

"You sound a little annoyed by that."

"Not annoyed. Just...I don't know. I thought I built her up in my head." *Nope.* She was even more gorgeous than he remembered. "I don't know what to say to the kid. To Lucas." Even saying his name out loud was weird.

"Just let things happen organically. And remember it'll be weird for them too. This is all new so it's not like you're the only one feeling awkward."

"True."

"Did you see the text from B?" Rowan asked, thankfully changing the subject.

Ezra nodded. Bradford had sent him a text telling him to look out for an incoming email with contract stuff. "Yeah, I was planning to look over the new contract before showering but I'm sure it's all good anyway." When they'd all gotten out of the Marines, he, Rowan, Tiago and Bradford, aka B, had bought a bar together. The three of them had moved to New Orleans to establish this new branch of Redemption Harbor Security, but Bradford had remained at the main office in North Carolina and still oversaw their co-owned bar. "I feel like we should all increase his share so he's the majority partner."

"I was thinking the same thing," Rowan said, nodding. "Tiago too. We were just talking about that last night. Or we could tell B we're open to selling if he wants to. He's so busy with Hailey's crew it might be a relief for him to offload it."

"Let's plan a phone conference and go over everything, let him know there are options."

That settled, Ezra topped off his coffee then hurried upstairs. He rarely stayed here, what with it being a safe house, but it was nice to be around his crew, especially today when he felt as if he could crawl out of his skin.

They all left extra sets of clothes in one of the spare rooms, and for the most part, they all carried a duffel in their vehicles with extra clothes and weapons, because you just never knew what the day would bring.

After showering, dressing and ordering himself to get his shit together, he headed out. Berlin had still been sleeping, and even though he'd wanted to bang on her door, demand to know what she'd found out about Samuel Perry, he'd managed to contain himself.

He knew the cops were at least investigating and he'd already texted with Magnolia this morning so he knew she was safe. Soon though, he was going to find out everything about the asshole stalking his...his friend. The mother of his son.

Sighing to himself, he pulled up to her gate this time on his bike, pressed the buzzer. Almost immediately the gate opened, which made him hope she'd been waiting for him.

As he parked, he glanced around automatically, took in the visible cameras, made a note to add a few more, then pulled his phone out as it buzzed in his jacket pocket.

From Scarlett. *Just saw you arrive. Everything good?*

Yeah, just here for breakfast. See anything last night? He was pretty sure she'd have alerted him if so, but asked anyway. He was glad she'd checked in so quickly. It told him that she was indeed watching the place. Not that he'd doubted it, but still.

Nothing out of the ordinary. We're still sitting tight though. Having her house back so far is a plus as far as security goes. At least she doesn't have to worry about drive-bys on her house.

Even the thought of that made him ill, but he sent back a thumbs-up, then swung off the bike, headed for the front door.

The door swung open before he could even think about knocking or pressing the bell. Magnolia was dressed similarly to yesterday in loose, faded jeans and a soft-looking green sweater that did nothing to hide her curves. Her dark hair was down in big waves instead of piled on her head, and her blue eyes...were kind of wild-looking.

"Everything okay?" he murmured, stepping into the foyer.

"Yeah, I think I've put too much pressure on myself. On this morning." She shoved out a sigh.

"Well something smells good."

She laughed a little. "That's because I cooked everything. Literally everything. I don't know what's wrong with me."

"Nothing's wrong with you." Moving on instinct and a deep-seated need to comfort her, he pulled her into a hug, was so damn grateful that she didn't pull back. Not even for a second. Instead she buried her face against his chest and held him tight. He wrapped his arms around her, closed his eyes for a long moment. He'd always loved holding her in his arms. Something about having her pressed up against him had always grounded him, made him feel like he could do anything.

He savored holding her, and for a moment it was as if he'd been dropped back in time as her familiar vanilla-lavender scent wrapped around him. "You still smell the same."

She laughed lightly and leaned back to look up at him. "So do you. So...this morning is probably going to be weird, and that's okay?"

"Definitely," he murmured, his gaze falling to her mouth. Damn it, he had to stop looking at her mouth. Because then he wanted to claim it. Claim her. Then he wanted to strip— *Oh shit.* They were not alone. He was vaguely aware of movement at the stairs that led off the foyer, saw Lucas coming down in pajama pants and a T-shirt.

Magnolia must have heard him, or sensed him too, because she stepped back and turned to face him. "You're awake."

Lucas's gaze ping-ponged between the two of them as he shoved his hands into the pockets of his flannel pants. "Yep." He cleared his throat as he reached the bottom of the stairs.

"Ah, I'm Ezra, officially." Ezra wasn't sure if he should shake his hand or what.

Luckily Lucas held out his hand, seeming relieved, maybe that Ezra had started the introduction. "Lucas, which, yeah, you already know."

Ezra found himself smiling as Magnolia ushered them toward the kitchen.

"Wow Mom, you cooked...a *lot*."

"I guess I went a little overboard." Her cheeks flushed a familiar shade of pink, and oh, Ezra had to shut down the direction of his thoughts.

There were scrambled eggs, bacon, sausage, croissants, a big bowl of mixed fruit, yogurt, cinnamon rolls, cereal, milk of various kinds (regular, oat, almond), orange juice and some sort of green juice that Lucas poured for himself. Oh, and a big pot of coffee.

"Help yourself," she said to Ezra, her cheeks flushing again as she went to get a bowl and fill it with fruit.

Even though he wasn't exceptionally hungry, she'd gone to a lot of trouble so he piled his plate with food. Luckily Lucas did the same.

The kitchen table was by a window overlooking the backyard. From this angle, it was a security nightmare, something he'd noticed yesterday while waiting on her to talk to Mari, then her parents. There was so much greenery, flowers, fruit trees and other foliage that anyone could sneak in using cover. Yep, he needed to increase her cameras back there too.

"Did you arrive on a motorcycle?" Lucas asked as they all got settled. "I heard the engine."

"Yeah, it's the new Ducati." He had a vintage Harley he'd restored as well, but figured now wasn't the time to talk about it.

"Very nice. I wanted to get one when I turned sixteen but my mom said I had to wait."

"That sounds very wise."

Lucas lifted a shoulder, shot his mom a grin. "Yeah. I'm going to wait until I'm in college. It'll be easier to get around town on one anyway."

Magnolia made a little sighing sound. "I don't even want to think about you leaving."

"Have you started thinking about college yet or is it too soon?" Ezra asked.

Lucas laughed lightly. "It's not too soon. We started ACT prep courses in ninth grade." He rolled his eyes at that.

Magnolia's mouth simply pulled into a thin line as she shot Ezra a knowing look. But he wasn't sure he understood the look because there was so much he didn't understand about Lucas's life.

"What colleges are you looking at?" he asked, because that seemed like a safe enough topic.

"I'm planning to apply to about six, including Tulane." He shot his mom a look.

"I didn't say anything." She turned her smile on Ezra. "I obviously want him to stay close to home, but I'm trying not to influence his decision. Even if it's hard," she added. "And Tulane has an incredible architecture program. We've scheduled a few college tours in the spring..." She looked at Lucas again and they seemed to have a silent conversation that ended with her nodding before she turned to Ezra. "If your schedule allows it, we'd love for you to come to some of the tours."

"Yeah," Lucas said, nodding.

Oh wow, he hadn't been expecting that at all. Hell, he hadn't been sure what to expect. "I'd love to. Sometimes my schedule is a lot, but I'll make time."

"So what do you do exactly?" Lucas asked around a mouthful of eggs.

"I'm a security specialist." His standard answer. "I work for a company that has a few different branches, but mainly we specialize in keeping individuals safe as well as analyzing the security for companies or individuals." They did a lot of gray area stuff not listed on their website like rescue kidnap victims independently of law enforcement or help abused women escape bad situations, and they'd taken down a handful of trafficking rings. But that wasn't up for public consumption.

"Cool. And you're now living here?"

"Yeah. For the last few months."

"And you didn't know..." Lucas cleared his throat, looked down at his food.

Okay, so it was on to real stuff. "I had no idea about you. I assumed your mom..." He shot Magnolia a quick look, got a nod so he took that to be a good sign. "I assumed your mom was happily married to someone else and I had no idea whether she had kids or not. I never…looked you up," he murmured, turning to Magnolia again. It had been too painful to even contemplate so he'd locked down that part of his life. "But I'm sorry for all the years we've lost. And I don't want to force anything on you, I'd just like to get to know you."

Lucas nodded, an easy smile on his face. "I want to get to know you too. And maybe you'll let me ride your bike."

He started to say yes, but then glanced at Magnolia.

She simply sighed. "That'll probably be fine."

"I built another one from the ground up," Ezra continued, looking at Lucas again. "I don't know if that idea interests you, but maybe we could work on one—"

"Yeah, that would be awesome." He shoveled more food in his mouth, eating at an impressive pace.

The rest of breakfast was smooth, or Ezra thought it was, then Lucas looked at his mom, his expression a little nervous. "I'm supposed to shoot hoops with some friends this morning, but I wasn't sure if that's a good idea?"

"Ah…"

"I've got two security pros watching your house. One of them can shadow you wherever you want to go, but indoors and familiar locations would be best. Somewhere like the Y where you need a pass to get in. Just no big public places with a lot of exits."

They both looked at him, blinked. So maybe that was a weird thing to say?

"How trained are they?" Magnolia asked.

"Most from their company are former military, not necessarily US military, but all trained in various weapons, self-defense, hand-to-hand combat, and offense tactics. I'd want them shadowing me," he added.

"Then I want them watching my mom." Lucas shook his head slightly. "I'll just stay here."

"I'll be shadowing your mom today," Ezra said before he could stop himself. He wasn't letting Magnolia out of his sight.

Magnolia's gaze narrowed slightly. "This is the first I'm hearing about that."

He lifted a shoulder. "I'd planned to tell you when I got here. So here I am, telling you."

Her eyebrow raised. "Not ask me?"

Lucas smothered a laugh, shoved more food in his mouth.

Ezra cleared his throat. "I feel like asking would be insincere. Because I'll be tailing you if you leave your house."

She gave him a look he wasn't sure how to define. She definitely wasn't angry, but she also wasn't amused. "Okay. You can run around with me today. And Lucas...I'm okay with you going to play basketball but only because it's at Jensen's house, right?"

He nodded.

"Okay, then you'll have to take Ezra's security person. And no side trips."

Lucas nodded. "That's fine. Thanks. Just...be careful. This guy has been threatening *you*."

"I know, and I'm always careful," she said.

Ezra begged to differ. He'd been there before she'd almost been shot and she hadn't been paying attention to anything.

"Would you mind if security drove you?" Ezra asked. "It would make things easier and you'd be in a different vehicle than your own." So if someone was watching their house, they wouldn't necessarily know it was Lucas leaving.

"Yes, that works," Magnolia said before Lucas could answer, seeming almost relieved by it.

Nodding, Lucas took his plate to the sink, then hurried out of the room saying he needed to shower.

"Sorry if I overstepped any boundaries," Ezra said once it was just the two of them.

She snorted softly as she started putting away the food. "You don't sound very sorry."

He stood and joined her, started loading up the dishwasher with the empty plates and glasses. "If I'm being totally honest, I'm not. I want you guys safe and this is my area of expertise. If I had my way, both of you would be in a safe house."

But he knew how that would go over. He had absolutely no say over their lives so he was trying to play this as right as possible.

"I don't even know if I should let him leave today," she said, leaning against the countertop, rubbing her hands over her face. "So far all the threats I've received have been personal, about me only. And yesterday..." She shuddered. "That was clearly directed at me. But he's everything to me. I just don't know what the right decision is."

"What's this Jensen's place like?"

"His family owns a mansion, has their own tennis and basketball court. So there's no public access. It's just going to be him and his friends."

He'd forgotten the difference in their social circles. He had wealthy friends (and yeah, he was doing okay for himself too), but they were in different stratospheres. "And Lucas's security... Would it make you feel better to talk to the security team?"

"Yes." She'd answered before he'd even finished asking.

He pulled out his phone and made the call.

CHapter 10

Scarlett stood at attention as she talked to Magnolia, all hard lines and edges. Next to her, Magnolia was slender, but she was soft and...goddammit, perfect.

Since when had Ezra gotten in the habit of comparing women? Never. Turning away, he stalked from the foyer into the living room, stood next to the front window. The Christmas tree glittered next to him, bright and cheery, with presents tucked underneath. There were multiple stockings on the fireplace mantel, including theirs, her parents', and one for Mari, which told him they must have people over on Christmas morning. Or maybe they had Christmas lunch here. The pang in his chest was sharp and he looked away, turning to the window instead. He'd missed a lot of years, something he was trying not to dwell on. But it was hard when the past was slapping him in the face.

"Are you sure it's okay for me to leave today?" Ezra turned at the sound of Lucas's voice.

He'd heard him coming down the stairs, and seen him in the reflection of the window, but hadn't been sure Lucas was coming to talk to him. "I don't love it, but given where you'll be and your security, it's okay. Do you want my phone number too?" He felt weird asking, but now was as good a time as any.

"Oh yeah, of course." Lucas pulled out his phone and quickly programmed it as Ezra gave it to him. Then he glanced over his shoulder, stepped a little closer and lowered his voice. "You'll be with my mom all day?"

"I'm not leaving her side." Unless it was in a body bag, but he kept that to himself. No one was getting to her.

Lucas nodded, shoved his hands into his shorts pockets. It was cold outside and the kid was wearing shorts, a T-shirt and a zip-up hoodie. Yeah, that sounded about right.

"So how long were you guys...like, together?"

Ezra blinked, surprised by the question, but it made sense Lucas would want to know. "A year."

He nodded again, glanced over his shoulder again. Not that he needed to bother—the low murmur of Magnolia and Scarlett's voices were still clear.

"Did you..." He cleared his throat.

Ezra wasn't sure where he was going, but he had a guess. "Did I love her? Yes. Very much."

Again with the nod, then followed by a look of frustration. "I'm so pissed at my grandpa. I can't believe... I can't understand why he did that."

Oh, this was tricky, because Ezra had a lot of anger at Magnolia's father, but he knew if he let that spill over, it wouldn't do anyone any good. "What he did was wrong, but he loves your mom. And parents aren't perfect." His certainly hadn't been—the understatement of the year. "He was trying to keep his daughter safe from what he thought was...a threat, I guess." Or more accurately, Ezra hadn't fit the mold of what Arnold Lavigne wanted for his daughter.

"My mom would never do anything like that to me."

"No, she wouldn't." Of that Ezra was certain. It didn't matter that he hadn't been in her life in years; that simply wasn't the type of person she was.

"Okay," Magnolia said, stepping into the living room, a too-bright smile on her face. "You're good to go. Just keep your phone on you," she added.

"I will." Lucas hugged and kissed his mom on the cheek, then turned to Ezra. "I might text you later if that's okay?"

Ezra nodded, something warm expanding in his chest. "Yeah, anytime."

"Just be glad he's actually got a cell phone now," Scarlett said with a grin. "When he was in the Marines, he didn't have a cell phone until his last year."

"No way." Lucas glanced at Ezra, eyes wide.

Ezra shrugged. He'd ditched his phone after everything with Magnolia had imploded—well, what he'd thought had happened. He'd always been with one of his friends anyway and there'd been a landline at the barracks. He hadn't seen the point.

"Yep," Scarlett said. "I've got a lot of stories about him if you're interested."

"PG ones only," he said mildly.

And Scarlett just grinned, then nodded once at Magnolia. "I'll keep your boy safe."

Once they were gone, Magnolia sagged a little. "I know she's trained, and honestly, she's a little scary, but I'm already questioning myself."

"I don't think he'll push back if you want him to stay home."

"I know he won't. He's such a good kid. But he's got finals next week and...he's been working so hard. So what were you guys talking about? If you don't mind me asking."

She could ask him anything, something she clearly didn't realize. "He was asking about you and me. From before."

She blinked in surprise. "Oh. Oooh. I guess I should have expected that." She sat on the love seat so he sat across from her in the chair by the Christmas tree. "He never pushed me about you. His father. And I thought... Well, truthfully I was just glad I didn't have to have the conversation. I've had enough awkward ones over the years as it is." She sighed and leaned back on the couch. "God, I'm so mad at my dad." Then she cleared her throat. "Sorry, you don't want to hear all that. And I can't even imagine how angry you must be."

He gave a short nod. "I'm trying to see it from his perspective. But yeah. It's a lot."

Her jaw tightened, but then all the air seemed to deflate from her. "I don't even want to think about him right now. I've got some work stuff to handle. A short meeting in a couple hours."

"Why on a Saturday?"

She gave him a wry smile. "The man I'm meeting with is high-maintenance, to put it lightly. Or as Lucas would say, a douche canoe."

Ezra let out a startled laugh.

"So...I need to tell you something and I know it's just going to add fuel to the fire, but I talked to my mom this morning. Apparently my dad did send that fake wedding invitation." She swallowed hard. "I'm sorry. I seriously don't know what he was thinking. He's been...well, he's been amazing since Lucas was born so it's hard to reconcile that he split us up. I know he did, but..." She sighed again, giving him a look he couldn't define.

"People are complicated."

"Yes, they are. Complicated assholes," she muttered, making him laugh again. She stood, looking restless. "I need to finish cleaning up the kitchen, then get ready—"

"I've got the kitchen. Go do what you need to do."

"You're sure?"

"Yep. Though you look good to me." He shrugged. Good, edible, same difference. God, she was heartbreakingly gorgeous.

She glanced down at her jeans, then back up at him and smiled. "Thanks. I won't be long."

"We're on your timetable today." He didn't care how long she took.

As he cleaned up her kitchen, Berlin called.

"Why didn't you wake me?" she said as he answered.

"You're mad that I didn't bang on your door this morning?"

"Well no, but you could have woken me." She sniffed slightly. "Anyway, I've got the lowdown on Samuel Perry, including a list of his priors. He's a nasty piece of work. The cops have a warrant out for his arrest but can't find him. I've added his face to our facial rec software so if he pops up anywhere in the city, we'll have him. I've added another layer of sensitivity to the cameras and CCTVs in and around Magnolia's office, the hotels her company reps, and her home cameras. The ones on her home are okay but I think we should add better cameras with more sensitivity."

"Agreed. She'll be out today but set it up, get someone over here. I'll let her know."

"Will do. And I've sent you a file to look at with all Perry's details. His ex is lucky to be away from him."

"What about security for her?" Because if he wanted Magnolia dead, he'd likely want his ex-wife dead too. Freaks like that had the whole "If I can't have her, no one can" mentality.

"Already took care of that. She's actually living at one of the hotels she's working at now. They've got a small wing for staff housing. I don't know for sure, but I'm guessing it's for this reason, or at least part of it. Women escaping their abusers have a safe place to work and sleep at night. According to the security notes I hacked, all employees have seen his picture and security has him marked as high alert, and to call the police if he shows up."

"At least they're taking his threat level seriously. What about known associates?"

"All in the file I sent you."

"Right. Thanks."

"So...how was breakfast?"

"Good. Really good." And he found himself cautiously optimistic that he could have a relationship with his son. It was still way too soon to know, but he was still optimistic. "I'll be with Magnolia all day, and Scarlett is with Lucas."

Berlin snort-laughed. "At least you know he's safe with that crazy bitch."

He laughed lightly. "Your words, not mine."

"*Accurate* words. So what's the plan? You sticking with her until this is over?"

"Yep."

"Good. We just got a call about a potential job, but nothing huge. As of now, we're not planning on taking on anything big until we've found this Perry guy. And it goes without saying that if you need backup, we're all here."

"Thanks. But I've got this. It's mainly just personal security until Perry is found." Or Ezra killed Perry. *Potato, potahto.* And he wasn't letting anyone else shadow Magnolia. That was all him.

"All right, well I've got my cell on me. If anything pops up on the feeds about

Perry, I'll let you know."

Once they disconnected, he finished cleaning up the kitchen right as Magnolia stepped into it, looking like she always did. Perfect. Instead of the casual jeans and sweater, she had on wide leg cream-colored pants, a striped black and cream top under a fitted black jacket, heels and accents of gold jewelry.

"You look ready to take on the douche canoe."

She laughed, the musical sound wrapping around him. "This guy is so annoying, but he's a brilliant architect and I really want his designs for a bid I'm planning to make. Unfortunately he knows how bad I want him and my competitor does too. I'm pretty sure he's dragging things out with both of us. I'm this close to walking."

"I have a few friends I can reach out to, see if they can help you grease this guy's wheels—or more likely offer up a different option."

"Thank you, but...I've got this handled. I'm just being whiny," she said on a laugh.

He lifted a shoulder and grabbed his jacket from the kitchen chair. "The offer will stand anyway. My friend's husband, Jesse Lennox, has recently bought up some real estate here so I'm sure he knows architects you could work with."

Magnolia blinked once. Twice. "Wait, Jesse Lennox the billionaire? The only billionaire who's known for real philanthropic work?"

"Yeah."

She grinned at him as she grabbed her keys from a little hook on the wall. "That's wild that you know him. And fine, maybe I'll take you up on it if I can't get this guy to decide who he wants to work with."

His gaze flicked down to her keys and he frowned.

"Oh, I'm driving, Ezra. Unless you plan on zooming us around town on your bike?"

He grinned at her tone, far too pleased to hear his name on her lips. "Fair point. I'll pick up a company vehicle later."

She'd started to respond when her phone buzzed. She frowned down at the screen. "That's weird. I rarely get deliveries here. I have everything sent to the office."

He leaned in, looked at the small feed on her phone showing the box sitting outside her gate, a delivery driver jumping back into his truck.

"You're not touching that box," he growled as instinctive protectiveness kicked in.

Her blue eyes widened. "It's probably something Lucas ordered."

"I don't care."

Her eyes widened even more.

"What?" he asked as he pulled up the detective's phone number, called her.

"You're just very bossy."

"I'm also not wrong... Detective, I'm at Ms. Lavigne's house. She's just received a suspicious package—"

"Don't touch it. I'm sending the bomb squad there now." Detective Flores's voice was sharp.

He hadn't been sure of her response, but was glad for it. They were clearly on the same page. "Okay. We're inside and not going anywhere."

As soon as they disconnected, he texted Scarlett's partner, Devi, and let them know not to come close to the box or the driveway.

"The bomb squad seems like a lot." Magnolia worried her bottom lip as he pocketed his phone.

"Better safe than sorry." Ezra hoped he was overreacting. That was the best-case scenario. The worst... He didn't even want to think about that.

CHAPTER 11

I'm still waiting for those tacos.

Magnolia wrapped her arms around herself as she watched through her living room window, very aware of Ezra's presence next to her. The man was impossible to ignore anyway.

Not that she wanted to ignore him, but that was something no mere mortal could do.

"Everything about this sucks," she muttered, watching as the bomb squad picked up the box with their robot, then slowly put it inside another big container thing.

"I know," he murmured. "I've already checked in with Scarlett. Lucas is safe and playing basketball. She sent me a couple pictures of him. I hope that's okay." His voice took on a quality she couldn't define.

"Of course it's okay." She looked up at him and couldn't get a read on his expression either. "You're his dad."

"I know. Well, I know that biologically I am but this is all surreal. I...thought about saving the picture as my screen saver but then thought it might be weird."

A rush of tears shoved up fast and hard so she turned back to the window. "That's not weird," she rasped out. "It's sweet." Jesus, this man had the ability to completely unravel her. Apparently some things hadn't changed.

She jumped as the ground shook slightly. "Oh my god, did they... Was that..."

"Yep. It was an explosive device." His voice was tight, controlled. Angry. "And I know I'm jumping ahead, but these two acts of violence are back-to-back. This kind of escalation is really, really bad, Magnolia."

"I know," she whispered, looking up at him again.

"I think you and Lucas should stay in a safe house."

"Okay."

Surprise flickered in his gaze for a moment. "Okay, then. Pack what you need for at least a week for you and Lucas. I can have someone stay here, someone trained, to keep an eye on your place if you're okay with that."

"If you trust them, I do." She glanced back outside to see Camila hustling down her driveway. "Come on," she murmured, breaking away from the window to greet her friend.

Ezra was faster, opening the front door before she could.

Camila nodded once at him, then stepped inside, pulled her into a quick hug. "That was quick thinking, calling us."

"Well you can thank Ezra." Magnolia nodded to him.

Camila gave him a curious look. "How exactly do you two know each other?"

"He's Lucas's father," Magnolia said before he could respond. "And we're going with him to a safe house."

Camila did a slow blink, then a slow sort of nod. "Ooookay, then. I'm glad to hear that. I know that he, and his company, will keep you safe. I'd planned to suggest you stay somewhere else for the time being so that's something out of the way. We're still looking for Perry, but he hasn't popped up on any cameras around town. He's either in disguise or he's gone to ground."

Magnolia simply nodded as Camila continued for a few more minutes. She was grateful for how seriously the PD was taking this, but she wanted to pack and get out of here. And she loved her house, was beyond angry that someone was driving her out of it.

But at the end of the day, her son's safety was the most important thing. She headed upstairs while Ezra talked with Camila, feeling on autopilot as she gathered their things. She knew what Lucas would need for the next week, including his backpack and books—he only had one exam left since he'd either finished the others early or had been able to opt out of others with final projects instead.

As she gathered all his stuff, she picked up a canvas painting the size of a small square shower tile tucked into his gym bag. She'd never seen it before, but it didn't look manufactured. Maybe he'd bought it at Jackson Square, or more likely at one of the smaller local art fairs. Or...maybe it was a gift from someone?

The painting was of the back of a man and woman, their heads tilted together, their arms wrapped around each other. The man had dark hair, the woman wavy red hair, and the background was a starry night. She wasn't sure what to make of this, set it back in his duffel, then quickly packed up what she thought he'd need. If she missed anything, they could send someone back for it.

By the time she made it downstairs, Camila had left and Ezra was talking to someone on the phone as he paced in the living room.

"I'll call you back," he growled before he stalked to the bottom of the stairs, plucked the duffel bag and her rolling suitcase from her. "I'd have helped with these."

"I know." Though she hadn't even thought about it. She'd barely dated since Lucas had been born. When Lucas had been about seven, she'd tried to dip her toes back into dating, but she hadn't been impressed with what was out there.

She'd heard the stories from her friends, but experiencing the nightmare of bad dates hadn't been worth the effort. After a man had gotten so sloppy drunk at a gala with her he'd had to be hauled out by security, she'd shelved all thoughts of dating. She'd been a busy mom and trying to prove herself at work, and men hadn't been worth the effort. So she'd thrown herself into those two things instead of trying to date on top of that.

"I've talked to my crew and the safe house is set up. I actually stayed there last night so I knew it was ready, but I wanted to check with them."

"You stayed there last night?"

"Yeah."

"You don't have a place in the city?"

"I do. I just didn't want to go home to it," he said bluntly.

"Oh." She didn't know how to interpret his tone. Or maybe she did and just didn't want to ask questions. So she changed the subject. "I need to let my parents know what's going on. Even if I don't want to deal with my dad right now, I need to talk to my mom and fill her in. And if you think I could swing it, I'd like to keep my meeting. The guy I was supposed to meet with texted me while the bomb squad was here." Words she'd never thought she'd say. "And he asked to move our meeting to lunch. What do you think?"

He was silent for a long moment instead of saying no, which surprised her. She could see him actively thinking. Finally he said, "If you let me set the meeting place and don't mind a couple of my people watching you. They'll be at a different table and the person you're meeting won't know we're there."

She blinked.

But he continued. "Also, I need the name of who you're meeting with so one of my coworkers can run his information, make sure he's not the psycho targeting you."

She blinked again. "You're very thorough."

"I'd be pretty bad at my job if I wasn't thorough." His gaze dropped to her mouth as he said the last word.

And oh. Ooohhh, she had memories of exactly how thorough he'd been once upon a time. She cleared her throat once. Twice. Finally she just nodded because words weren't happening.

"I'm gonna need the guy's name." His mouth quirked up slightly and she had no doubt he knew his effect on her.

Because some things definitely hadn't changed.

"Louis Tremblay. And I'll text him, tell him where we're going to meet. What place should I pick?"

He rattled off a local place she'd heard of but never visited. Then said, "It's small and will be easy for us to watch the exits. Also, we know the owner so we can be open about what's going on. And I've asked one of my crew to drop off an SUV for us to use. That way we're not driving around in your vehicle. I've already checked it for tracking devices, but this keeps down the possibility of someone seeing you by chance."

"Thank you for doing this. Seriously, it sounds like a lot. And whatever I owe your company—"

"Magnolia." The way he said her name had far too many emotions packed into that one word.

"What?"

"I'm doing this to keep you and Lucas safe. You're not paying me." And he sounded almost offended that she was offering.

She stepped forward, closing the short distance between them, resisted the urge to touch him. "I wasn't trying to offend you. This is just a lot of trouble you're going to."

He shoved out a sigh. "I know, and you didn't offend me. But I haven't been able to take care of either of you for years. I'm trying to make up for it."

"You don't need to make up for anything either."

"Well I'm doing this. So just accept it," he said.

She found herself grinning despite the shit show her life had turned into. "And you say I'm the bossy one."

That got a smile out of him, and whew, her hormones, which had been dormant for so long they had cobwebs, flared to life. That smile was absolutely everything. It was the reason her teenage self had agreed to go on a date with him. That, and his motorcycle.

Oh, she was in trouble. "And thank you again for making this happen."

He shrugged. "I know it's important to you."

Yep. So. Much. Trouble.

CHAPTER 12

*Don't ask questions you don't want the
answer to.*

Ezra covertly watched Magnolia from the bar where he sat with Tiago at one of
his favorite Greek restaurants. They'd helped the owners with a problem four
months ago so the couple had been more than happy to let them use this place
for the meeting. They'd even given Magnolia the best table. It had a view of the
courtyard, but was still private enough that no one could sneak up on them.

Not that he'd let that happen anyway.

Rowan and Adalyn were at the table next to Magnolia's, not appearing as
if they were paying attention at all. The seating was spaced out so no one felt
crowded, and there was room for privacy.

Not that the two men were being quiet at all. Louis Tremblay, the architect
she was trying to work with, had a loud, braying laugh. And Magnolia's cousin,
Charles Barbier, who'd she'd brought in for this meeting because he knew Tremblay on a personal level, also had a booming laugh. Though it was clear he was
just as frustrated with Tremblay as Magnolia.

Oh, they were both hiding it well, but the eyes didn't lie.

"Your woman is a boss," Tiago murmured, his gaze flicking to the mirror
behind the bar.

They'd been using it to covertly keep tabs on the table. Berlin was in the parking lot, keeping an eye on the back exit in person, and she'd hacked into the private security feed to keep an eye on the front door. "She's not my woman."

Tiago simply snorted. "Whatever you've got to tell yourself."

They weren't using earpieces for this since it was such a small job. Berlin was sending them random texts to check in, but that was it. So he didn't have to worry about the others overhearing them. Still, Ezra didn't rise to the bait, knowing exactly what his friend was trying to do. "So how's your secret project going?"

Tiago was quiet for a long moment, then said, "Good. I think. But we need your help."

He glanced at him, putting his fork down. "With what exactly?"

"Rowan and I bought a plane."

He blinked. "What?"

"It's a little four-seater Cessna. It's in good shape, but we need to do some work on it and bit off more than we thought. Rowan wanted to surprise Adalyn with it which is why I haven't been able to tell Fleur. I didn't want to ask her to keep a secret from Adalyn. Plus I'm pretty sure they tell each other everything anyway."

"I've never worked on a plane before."

"Yeah, but you've worked on engines in general before. We've already talked to a guy, but I'd like you to come with us when he stops by and see if what he's saying makes sense. Basically make sure he's not trying to rip us off. Also we were hoping you might want to do some of the interior work. The seats need to be replaced or refurbished."

Ezra nodded. "I'll need to look at it, but yeah. I'll see if I can do the seats for you. If not, I'm sure I know someone who can."

Smiling now, Tiago nodded. "Thanks."

"So...a plane? Is this a Christmas present?"

"Sort of. We got it for a steal at forty thousand. It's more or less an investment. We can't always depend on Jesse or Brooks for use of their jets. Which are amazing, I'm not knocking them at all. But this is something that's a lot more low key, won't stand out at private airports. And we'll be able to get in more places undetected with something this small."

"That's really smart," he murmured.

"Exactly. And I'm going to get my private pilot's license. So's Rowan. You should do it with us."

"Seriously?"

"Sure, why not? Adalyn can already fly, but it'll be even better if more of us can. I think Berlin might be into it too, but she hasn't given us an answer either way."

"I'll think about it." He loved his bike—and having his feet on the ground. He was fine to fly, but didn't want to go out of his way to do it.

"I know what that means…" He trailed off, chin nodding to the table behind them.

Ezra glanced in the mirror, saw Tremblay standing.

Magnolia and her cousin stood as well, both shaking hands with him before Tremblay left. Then the two of them sat back down, shared a "look" and snickered. They talked for a few more minutes, then her cousin stood and left as well.

Magnolia waited a solid two minutes before she looked in his direction, then smiled, nodded him over.

He slid into the seat next to her. "So?"

"So…he's still jerking me around," she murmured, her smile never wavering. But he saw the frustration in her pretty blue eyes. "And if it's not too much trouble, could you reach out to your friend? If Jesse Lennox has contacts, I'm absolutely sure that the person I'm submitting a bid to won't lock himself into working solely with Tremblay." She paused, her expression a little savage as she smiled. "Plus it would be amazing to stick it to him. He thinks he's untouchable and is such a pain in the ass to work with. He loves getting all these free meals."

"It's not too much trouble," he murmured, pulling out his cell. He quickly texted Hailey, was surprised to receive a text back seconds later.

Of course. Whenever your girl wants, let me know. I'm sitting with him now. He's says to give her his personal cell phone.

Thanks. You're the best.

I know! And you also didn't negate the "your girl" so I know you're in deep. Then she sent a bunch of eggplant and peach emojis because of course she did.

Sighing, he sent Jesse's number to Magnolia to import. "Just sent you Jesse's personal cell number. Hailey said that he said to call anytime you'd like to talk."

Magnolia's eyes widened slightly. "Okay, I can't even pretend not to be impressed. So you're friends with Hailey Lennox?"

"Yeah, we served together. She was in Intel mostly, but bunked with us on occasion."

"I saw the announcement of their marriage. It was this big splash, but then there's been almost nothing since. Not that I'm looking up celebrities—and I'm not sure he counts as one. But I haven't seen anything about them."

"Yeah, that's intentional. He was really deliberate about 'leaking' the photos of their wedding to certain publications. He's incredibly protective of her." Something Ezra respected. "I honestly never thought I'd like anyone she ended up with. She was always like a little sister to us, but..." He shrugged. "He's one of the most generous people I've ever met. And he adores her."

"That's high praise. And for the record I have so many questions about what you've been up to the last seventeen years. I just don't want to bombard you with questions."

"I have a lot of questions too." Some he wasn't going to ask because he didn't want the answer. "But first let's get out of here and you can call Lennox and get the ball rolling on finding a new architect. How do you think your cousin will handle it?"

She shrugged and stood as he pulled out her chair. "Charles will be fine. He gets paid either way and he's just as annoyed with Tremblay as I am. The two of them play tennis and race sailboats together, have known each other forever—they went to the same prep school. Honestly I feel like Charles should have already closed this deal but..." She lifted a shoulder.

Ezra glanced down at his phone, saw a text from Berlin.

All clear.

"Okay, we're good to go." He saw another text pop up from Scarlett and let it sit until they were in the SUV. He missed his bike already—and wanted to take Magnolia for a ride just like old times, but knew now wasn't the time for that.

"Is everything okay?" Magnolia asked as he started the engine. "I saw Scarlett's name pop up."

"Yeah, she said that Lucas told her to hold off on going to the safe house."

She raised her eyebrows at that and pulled out her phone. To his surprise, she put it on speaker.

"Hey, Mom."

"Hey, hun. It's me and Ezra, you're on speaker. I hear you want to hold off on going to the safe house?"

There was a short pause. "I talked to Nana and she's really upset. I don't know why, but she's got it in her head that I'm going to like cut her out because Grandpa acted like an asshole."

"Lucas," she murmured, only slightly admonishing.

"After what he did..." He took a deep breath. "I don't want to talk about him. He's staying in the pool house anyway apparently. Nana is really, really mad. I've never even heard her curse before but she's the one who called him the stubborn asshole first. Anyway, I don't know, I wasn't sure if it was safe enough but I was hoping to go stay with her. But I also don't want to like, abandon you."

"Honey, you're not abandoning me. I'm just worried about your safety. Give me a sec, okay?" She muted the call, looked at Ezra.

"Their place is fine for him to stay at. Berlin already checked out their security, said it's a hell of a lot better than yours."

"Your 'tech person'?"

"Yep."

"Did she...hack their system?"

"I don't think I should answer that."

"Fine, but she and you think it's okay?"

"I wouldn't let him stay anyplace I was worried about. You'll need to talk to your mom and make it clear that no one is allowed over. Not even friends. And since he's got school on Monday, I don't want him driving his car to school. We'll need to provide one for him. Actually...I'd prefer that me or one of my people just drove him. I know he's almost seventeen but this is serious."

"All of this is fine, including having someone drive him. And my mom will be on board with anything. She'll do anything for Lucas or me."

He nodded then. "Okay, it's fine, then. Oh and she'll need to set the alarm during the day."

Magnolia nodded, then got back on the phone with Lucas and went over everything. Then as he headed for the safe house, she called her mom and went over the same thing.

That conversation sounded a lot more emotional, but it was clear that her mom had never been a part of anything. Which made him feel a lot better. He wanted to be in Lucas's life more than anything, a truth that had settled in his bones. He had a kid.

Who was almost a grown man. But still. Ezra wasn't just going to abandon him, and it mattered that Magnolia's mom was upset by what her husband had done too.

"I feel like my life is a soap opera," Magnolia murmured as she set her phone back in her purse. "But I feel good knowing he'll be with my mom. She'll spoil the heck out of him until he leaves for school Monday. And she'll convince him to prep for his test tomorrow."

Ezra smiled at her words, just enjoying being with her, even if the circumstances were the worst.

"So did you and Scarlett ever date?" she asked.

Beyond surprised by the question, he automatically tightened his grip on the steering wheel. "Ah, no. Why?"

Magnolia's cheeks were flushed pink, but she shrugged. "I was just curious. I haven't seen you in so many years and you have a very easy camaraderie with her. Is it weird that I asked?"

"No, not at all. She's not my type so it surprised me, that's all." Which wasn't exactly the truth. He was just surprised that she cared enough to ask. Either way he'd have told her if he was putting their son's safety in the hands of an ex.

"What is your type?" she blurted. "Never mind! Don't answer that. Jeez," she muttered, more to herself it sounded like as she turned away to stare out the window. "Sorry, I'm just up in my head right now."

He cleared his throat. "I've only ever had one type." Her.

She sucked in a little breath, but didn't look back at him. Which was probably just as well. Right now he needed to be completely focused. To keep her and their son safe at all times. And as soon as they got to the safe house, he was going to ask Berlin to hack into the security cameras at her parents' house so he could keep an eye on things and receive any alerts.

Besides, it made sense that she was curious about his romantic entanglements—none—because he was obsessed with knowing hers. But since he didn't want the answer, he wasn't asking. At least that was what he kept telling himself.

CHAPTER 13

"Oh my god, you put Nair in his shampoo?" Magnolia turned to Ezra, eyes wide, and was graced with one of his gorgeous smiles.

The kind that hit her right in the solar plexus, made it hard to breathe.

"I will neither confirm nor deny that." But his grin remained in place before he turned a dry look to Tiago. "And if we're telling stories, I've got a few I'm sure Fleur would love to hear."

"Oh yes, please!" Fleur pushed her plate back and picked up her glass of white wine. "I want to hear all the stories.

Fleur, who Magnolia knew through reputation only as a talented artist, had joined all of them for dinner at the safe house. Being surrounded by so many people normally would have stressed her out, but everyone was so nice and friendly. And it was clear they adored Ezra.

Magnolia was trying to keep everyone straight and was pretty sure she had it now. Berlin was the hacker of their group, a striking woman who was mostly dressed in black. Even her T-shirt, which had Kirby on the front, was mostly black. Adalyn and Rowan were recently married, Tiago and Fleur were engaged and still trying to decide on a venue, and then Ezra, who she had no problem remembering.

If anything, he was imprinted on the deepest part of her.

They also talked about other people including someone named "B," who they all owned a bar with. They'd also talked about people named Cash, Reese, Elijah and Hailey. Hailey was the only one she was positive about since she was Jesse Lennox's wife.

"No stories." Tiago gave Ezra a pointed look.

Ezra simply grinned again, leaned back and slung an arm around the back of Magnolia's chair. And oh, she liked that way too much. "Fine. And for the record, that asshole deserved the Nair. Sadistic bastard," he muttered in reference to a drill sergeant they'd all loathed.

A burst of laughter erupted from the table.

"I have a story about Ezra," Magnolia murmured, shooting him a grin.

He covered his face. "I don't even want to think about what you might tell them," he said, laughing lightly before grinning as he looked at her.

She loved seeing him so relaxed like this, so sure of himself, and found herself holding her breath for a second, as if she could somehow freeze this one moment in time. It would live in her memory at least. She'd started to tell one of her favorite stories when her phone buzzed. "Oh, saved by the bell. It's Lucas," she said to the others. "I need to take this. You want to come with me? We can do a video call?"

Ezra looked faintly surprised but stood with her, telling Tiago that he could handle the dishes tonight before they both headed out onto the back patio.

She answered, pressing the video option as they both sat on a swinging bench. She leaned in with Ezra as she held up the phone. "Hey, hon. You've got both of us."

Lucas smiled at them and she recognized the background immediately. He was in one of the guest rooms that was essentially "his" room, as her mother had dubbed it during his formative years. And it really was his room, having evolved with him in age. "Hey, just checking in to let you know everything is...okay over here. Nana's great. She's really mad." His eyes were big as he glanced over in the direction of the bedroom door then looked back at them, his voice lowered. "Nana's scary. I've never seen her mad before. Not like this anyway because it's a real kind of mad. She's like this silent, deadly terrifying Nana. Grandpa came in and she iced him out, didn't even offer him the tacos we made. I almost felt bad for him." His jaw tightened. "Almost."

"Are you sure you want to stay?"

"Yeah, we're going to watch a movie. I think she needs me right now."

"You're not responsible—"

"Mooom, I know, I know. I'm *not* responsible for anyone's happiness but that's not what this is. She's my Nana and I love her. I want to be with her right now and I think you and..." His gaze flicked to Ezra and he cleared his throat. "I think you two are good right now. She needs me more and maybe I need her too."

"You're a wonderful human being, in case I don't tell you that enough."

"Moooom." Again with the extended syllables, but he was hiding a smile.

She could tell. "Fine. Then I'll jump into mom mode. Are you ready for your test on Monday?"

"Yep. Nana's helping me study tomorrow. She said we could have tonight off and watch movies and eat junk food, then get serious tomorrow."

"Okay, I love you."

"I love you too." He looked at Ezra. "I might text you later, okay?"

"Definitely."

And that was it. Once they disconnected, she shoved out a sigh as she stared out at the yard full of solar lights and different pieces of yard art intertwined with the flowers, plants and trees. There were a lot of gnomes everywhere and they were delightful. "I hope I'm doing the right thing by letting him stay there."

"You're a good mom." His voice had dropped an octave.

Surprised, she glanced at him. "Thank you."

"I'm serious. You just... I'm pissed at your dad, not gonna lie. But maybe he was right. It's clear that you're killing it in the parent department. That kid, our son, is loved and knows it. Maybe..." He shrugged. "I don't know. I don't know where I would have fit in so maybe your dad had the right of it."

"Ezra Hunt. Don't you dare say that," she snapped. Then she grabbed his face and kissed him.

She surprised herself and started to pull back, but he clutched the back of her head, let out what she could only describe as a savage growl as he devoured her.

And that was really the only word for it as he teased his tongue against hers, took over what she'd started until they were both panting and staring at each other.

She blinked first. "I'm sorry," she whispered.

"Don't be sorry." His voice was gravelly, uneven. "We can't do it again, but...don't be sorry."

They couldn't do it again? Ooooh, yeah, that was definitely disappointment sliding through her. He was probably right, but she could admit that she didn't like to be told to do anything. Or *not* to do anything, as it were.

So he might as well have lit the pilot light of her desire and tossed a match onto it. "Okay, I'm not sorry. But you don't get to talk about yourself like that. Okay? We would have made things work. And my dad was wrong. So very wrong. So he doesn't get let off the hook. Okay?" she demanded.

"Okay."

Almost as if he knew she was talking about him, her phone buzzed with an incoming call from her dad. She silenced it.

Ezra's eyebrows raised.

"I'm not ready to talk to him yet."

"I get it," he murmured, then paused when Berlin stuck her head outside. "Sorry to bother you guys, but I wanted to talk to Ezra about some stuff."

"That's okay. I need to return some work emails anyway." Didn't matter that it was Saturday evening, Magnolia felt like she never really shut things down. Oh, she tried to keep a good work-life balance, and had made it to all Lucas's events growing up, but that meant sometimes she worked late nights or odd hours. Magnolia stood, hating the interruption as much as she was grateful for it.

Because she needed a little distance from Ezra after that kiss. She'd never thought she'd see him again, much less have this type of reunion. And he didn't want to do it again? She wanted to push him, but was pretty sure she didn't want the answer. For all she knew, he was dating someone else.

No...she didn't think so. But there was something more there holding him back.

***

"Are we gonna talk about that hot and heavy kiss?" Berlin asked as she sat in front of her computer.

"Uh, no *we* are not talking about that." Ezra glared at the back of her head. "Since when are you so nosy?"

"Figured I'd ask. Besides, I've got some gossip for you. Guess who's been leaving envelopes of cash for Antonia Collins then sneaking away?" Her fingers moved across the keyboard as quickly as he'd ever seen anyone. She texted the same way too. "I'll tell you who, Adalyn."

Yeah, he'd guessed that.

"You have nothing to say?" She glanced over her shoulder at him, pausing at the computer.

"I wasn't sure if you were done."

"Ha, ha."

"I don't know what to say to that. Does Collins know that Adalyn was leaving her money?"

"You can't call her by her last name. That's a dude thing."

"Well I've never met her in person so... Oh my god, Berlin. Answer the question."

She snickered then swiveled in her chair. "Yeah, she knows now. She dropped by this place before you got here last night. Told Adalyn she was coming to dinner on Sunday. Not asked, she ordered her. It was hilarious. I told Adalyn to bring Gumbo."

Hearing her name, Gumbo trotted into the room from who only knew where, yipped once at the two of them.

Ezra crouched down and rubbed behind her ears, letting the mutt headbutt him for more pets and more attention. Then Gumbo lay down on her back, shaking her entire body as she demanded more pets.

"I don't know if all dogs are like her, but she's so wonderfully weird," Berlin murmured. Then she straightened in her seat. "Anyway, the reason you're here.

I got a few hits on some of Perry's known associates. Nothing concrete but I managed to snag a few bits of phone conversation about a 'delivery' and how it didn't make its intended recipient. Could be a mention of the bomb. Or it could just be a reference to drugs, considering the guy in question sells drugs. But I wanted to let you know I'm still digging. And my baby," she said, caressing her laptop, "is working overtime."

"Thank you for this." He just wished he could get his hands on Perry and this problem would go away forever.

"I don't even want to know what you're thinking right now because you're looking kinda murdery. But I'll wake you if I get anything good." She grinned then, all mischievous Berlin. "Will you be in your room or Magnolia's?"

"Mine." His tone was dry as he stood, Gumbo deciding to remain behind. As he stepped out of the office, he watched the little goofball jump into Berlin's lap and start licking her face.

And despite what he'd said, he headed to Magnolia's room, knocked on the half-open door. They'd given her one of the biggest rooms, and he knew it had been decorated with comfort in mind. It was all soft grays and blues with a king-sized bed, a desk, cushy seating by the window that overlooked the backyard, and a giant soaker tub he'd heard about from Berlin. Because the woman talked about everything.

"You doing okay?" He stepped inside, resisted the urge to shut the door behind him and pick up where they'd left off on the back porch.

But there would be no picking up anything. Even if her taste, the little moaning sound she made, was imprinted on him. He hadn't been expecting her kiss at all, but when she'd grabbed his face like that something primal had unleashed in him. And if they'd been alone, he was pretty sure he'd have tossed out all his restraint and gone down on her right on the porch swing.

"Okayish." She'd changed into dark blue pajamas with little hearts all over them. "I talked to Mari and she always makes me laugh. And I talked to my mom for a few minutes. I'm not upset with her, but it was still hard because she's so understandably emotional. She's taking this really bad." She shook her head.

"Anyway. Okayish is not too bad."

He shut the door behind him now and stepped inside, sitting on the end of the bed. "You don't have to cut yourself off when talking about your dad."

"I know, but I don't want to treat you like a therapist or something. Especially when what he did affected you too."

"You can talk to me about him all you want. Your mom too. I want to know everything about how you're feeling. Hell, about all the years I missed."

"You want to look at pictures of Lucas? I've got a dedicated album on my phone. Unless...will it be too much?" She bit her bottom lip, and he loved and hated that she was worried about him.

"I'd love to see them." Yeah, it would hurt a little, but he wanted to know everything about his son.

"Good. Come on." She grabbed her phone and slid onto the big bed, sat up against the headboard. Then she patted the place next to her. "I won't bite...unless you ask nicely."

He blinked at her boldness, but didn't miss the pink flush of her cheeks. Laughing lightly (something he seemed to be doing a lot of with her), he slid in next to her, staying on top of the covers as she held out her phone.

"Just swipe right and I'll tell you about them if you have questions. To be fair, I'm only showing you his kindergarten and first grade year because if I show you all of them at once, we'll be here until the end of time itself."

He wouldn't mind that at all, but he simply started scrolling. And she hadn't been kidding. There were a lot. Some with her, some with Lucas and kids his age, his teachers, his grandparents, then a lot of solos of him doing random things at different places. There were pictures at the Audubon Aquarium, the zoo, what he assumed were field trips since one showed a dairy farm and a bunch of kids in matching uniforms. In all of them, he was smiling of course, but Ezra loved the ones with him and Magnolia.

"Can I get some of these?" he rasped out.

"You can have all of them. I was going to make you a book for each year." She yawned and leaned her head on his shoulder as he kept scrolling. "He was mad at me that day," she said when he scrolled to a picture at a white sand beach. "Didn't want to take any pictures, but then when I put the phone down, he got mad and said I must not love him if I wasn't taking pictures."

Ezra snorted.

"Oh yeah, the emotions of a six-year-old. He was just hangry, I realized after a big meltdown. That age was tough though. One day he loved peanut butter, then the literal next it was the most disgusting thing in the world and I was a monster for trying to feed it to him."

Ezra snickered.

"Forget terrible twos or threes. Six was a rough year. He got a little more even-keeled at seven."

Smiling, he kept scrolling, then paused at a picture with Henri Fontenot and Lucas, both wearing matching white suits.

"Ah, it was a parent thing at school," she murmured.

"A dad thing?"

"No, Thanksgiving," she said. "Henri came to a lot of events over the years."

"You have good friends. I'm glad you had that for you and Lucas." Being a single mom was no joke. His own mom had put up with her shitty husband because she'd hated being alone. Hated Ezra, he was pretty certain. His dad had died years ago, been killed in a barfight, no surprise. He hadn't even received the notice immediately because it had gone to an old address.

"Thank you. I was lucky, I know that. And privileged. I can only imagine how hard it would have been without my resources. My parents didn't want me to forgo college so they hired help, and helped out a lot themselves. Now I'm guessing my dad did so much out of guilt." A hint of anger laced her words.

"Maybe, maybe not. He loves you."

She just sniffed once. "Mari swore she wouldn't mind being roommates with a baby but I knew that was crazy so I lived at my parents until Lucas was five. When he started kindergarten and I was just out of college seemed like the best time for a new start for both of us. We lived in a great little condo that was family friendly until he was ten. And my parents still helped out a lot too, so even though I was a single mom, I had a big safety net. Something a lot of people don't."

"That's why you're trying to create a safety net for other moms," he murmured, setting her phone down.

"Moms and women in general. It's seriously scary how thin the line is between homelessness and having a roof over your head. We don't have enough safety nets so I'm doing what I can to mitigate that."

Yep, there was a reason he'd fallen for her. "I never stopped thinking about you," he said into the quiet even as he told himself to shut the hell up. But he wanted her to know. Even if there wasn't going to be a future between them, romantically at least, he wanted her to know on the deepest level. "But I never looked you up. I thought you were happily married and I didn't want to see that." His words were blunt, raw. *True.*

She reached over, squeezed his thigh once. "I know it's not my fault, but I'm still sorry."

He didn't want apologies from her, just to explain to her why he hadn't looked back. "I just thought you should know," he murmured before he eased back, sliding out of her bed. The voice in his head told him he was a fool for walking away, but he knew better. This was the only way to save himself. "If you need me, I'm next door."

She simply nodded, her expression one he couldn't read. Which was just as well. Because if she asked him to stay, he absolutely would. And right now, things were too tenuous between them. Too fragile.

He didn't want to blow things up and ruin his chance at being in their lives. Because if they got involved with each other again, then things imploded... He knew exactly how that would play out.

No way. He'd just found out he had a son, that Magnolia had never ended things. He wasn't going to lose them when he'd just found them.

CHAPTER 14

Magnolia held her finger up to her mouth as Gumbo sat down next to her, her tail wagging wildly. She was trying to eavesdrop, thank you very much, and didn't need the dog giving her away.

After a sleepless night, she'd come downstairs searching for coffee and heard Ezra talking with the others. Crouching down by the kitchen entrance, she petted Gumbo as Ezra talked quietly with his team. A team and company in general she had a lot more questions about.

"We can bring out a drone for this," Tiago said. "But I don't know if it's necessary for just recon."

"I think parabolic mics will be fine and we bring the drone for backup in case we can't get close enough," Ezra said.

"I say we take two vehicles," Berlin said. "That way if we need to hide a body, we can use one vehicle to dispose of him."

"I can't tell if you're joking," Tiago muttered.

"Pretty sure she's not." Ezra. "And I'm on board with that idea."

Magnolia's eyebrows shot up. She looked at Gumbo, who just licked her face.

"Jesus," Tiago muttered again. "We're not disposing of anything."

"Don't let her fool you into feeding her. She's already been fed." A voice behind her made her jump. Adalyn.

Feeling her face flush, she smiled up at Adalyn, not even a little sorry about eavesdropping. "I'll give her treats anyway."

The pretty redhead smiled. "You don't have to eavesdrop. Just go on in."

"You didn't have to narc me out," she muttered as she stood. In the kitchen Ezra and the other two were quiet as they walked in. "Are you guys serious about the body thing?"

"No!" Tiago said.

Ezra just shrugged. Berlin did the same.

Magnolia blinked. "I'm going to need coffee. Also, tell me what this recon thing entails."

Ezra grabbed a mug for her. "I've got your coffee. I saw how you make it at your house."

Oookay then, that gave her far too many feelings. She sat at the island top next to Berlin who had her laptop in front of her.

"I think I found out where Perry might be. One of his known associates has been texting a burner phone and it sounds like the guy might be helping Perry hide in exchange for some low-level transport. AKA moving drugs in and out of the city."

"When are we leaving?" she asked as Ezra set her coffee, just the way she liked it, in front of her. "Thank you." She smiled up at him, wishing he'd stayed the night with her last night. Not that it had even been on the table for him. Then she wouldn't have tossed and turned all night and woken up unsatisfied.

"Weee?" Berlin stretched the word out slowly.

"Uh, yeah. You said it's just recon and you guys are not leaving me here."

Ezra cleared his throat and she could see the indecision in his eyes.

"Is it dangerous?" she asked.

"We're just trying to get eyes on him. That's all. It's not dangerous."

"What happens if you see him?"

"Then we call Detective Flores and let her know so she can let the correct people know to execute the warrant for him."

"Like I said, when do we leave?" She lifted her mug to her mouth.

Berlin cleared her throat and Adalyn simply grinned. Tiago avoided eye contact with all of them so Magnolia looked at Ezra.

He sighed. "We're ready now. You're riding with me."

She slid off the stool. "Ready to go." Then she looked at Berlin. "Can you send me some of those files you have on Perry? I'm curious about what you found."

"Ah...sure?"

"Thanks." Magnolia smiled at her, then up at Ezra.

He was definitely annoyed, or maybe just frustrated, but he grabbed another travel mug and headed for the garage. He was silent until they got in one of the SUVS, then when they pulled out, he finally spoke. "I wasn't being serious about...killing Perry."

"Okay." But she wasn't so sure. It was the main reason she'd wanted to come this morning. Plus she'd wanted to be with Ezra and see what he did for a living. But he'd sounded serious and she wasn't going to let him throw away his life over garbage like Samuel Perry. "So how does this work?"

"What do you mean?" he asked as he pulled onto a main road.

It was early enough on Sunday that the traffic was thinner than normal. "Do you guys really use drones to spy on targets? Is that what you call them?"

His mouth quirked up slightly. "Yes and yes. Sometimes we use something as simple as binoculars. Or one of us plants bugs. But this is supposed to be a house in a suburban-type neighborhood so we're going to keep it simple."

"And not kill him," she added.

He slid his sunglasses on as he took the ramp to the highway leading east. "No one's killing anyone. Probably."

***

Magnolia yawned and leaned her seat back a few more inches.

"You're the one who wanted to come," Ezra murmured, a hint of laughter in his voice.

"I know. I just thought a stakeout would be more exciting." But the last three hours they'd been sitting in the parking lot of a small public park across the street from some random guy's house in the hopes that Perry would show up.

It hadn't been all bad. She'd enjoyed talking to Ezra, but...yeah, this was boring. "So are all stakeouts like this?"

"Mostly."

"Oh my god, you're lying."

He grinned at her now. "I'm not lying! Most stakeouts are like watching paint dry. But some are exciting."

"How'd you end up in this line of work anyway? And what does your team really do? Because none of you act or even dress like the security people I've worked with before. Even Scarlett was in a suit and had a certain look to her."

"I sort of fell into it. Hailey asked me and the others if we wanted to bring down assholes and have fun doing it—her *exact* words—and get paid on top of it. She said we'd get to kick in doors and make bad guys cry on the regular."

Magnolia snorted out a laugh. "She sounds amazing."

"Her weapon of choice is bear spray. She buys it in bulk, and I'm not kidding. She's made more grown men cry than I can count. She is *very* liberal with it."

Magnolia started laughing. "Oh my god. I shouldn't be laughing but that's amazing. Mari carries bear spray too! She says it's the best defense. I should start carrying bear spray around."

He grinned. "I think that's a great idea. So yeah, we're not typical security. Our mission is literally all about helping people who need it the most. People who can't pay or don't have anywhere else to turn to."

Oooh, like she needed more reasons to adore him. "That's amazing."

Another shrug. *Gah, this man.*

"So...I think Lucas might be dating someone and not telling me."

He shot her a surprised look. "Why do you say that?" he asked before turning back to watch the house across the street.

It was cold out so there weren't any kids at the park. Or maybe because it was still early and Sunday. Cars had been coming and going from the one-story ranch-style house all morning. The people arriving had walked in the open garage, then walked out less than ten minutes later. She knew that Berlin and Tiago were taking pictures with a long-range camera to get shots of the license plates. She had no idea what they were going to do with them. Maybe give them to Camila? Or maybe that was wishful thinking on her part.

"I don't know. I found this little painting in his duffel bag when I was packing up. I wasn't snooping," she added, feeling the need to defend herself even though he wasn't remotely judging her. "He's always been open with me. I mean, I gave him 'the talk,' and while it was awkward, I don't know, I feel like I did all right. And whenever he's had a question, I've always tried to be honest. I don't know why he wouldn't tell me if he was dating someone."

Ezra was quiet for a long moment. "It might not be about you. Or his relationship with you. It could just be he doesn't know how he feels about this hypothetical relationship yet. And he's still young, figuring shit out." He shrugged. "If he is dating someone and hasn't told you, I don't think it's a reflection of his relationship with you or how he views you."

"Yeah, I guess." She sighed. "He's just growing up so fast and soon he'll be moving out. I'm not ready for it."

Reaching over, he picked up her hand, laced his fingers through hers and squeezed. He didn't say anything else, was just a solid comfort. He'd been like that seventeen years ago before everything had gone pear-shaped. It was comforting that he was still seemingly the same.

Then that sense of sadness swept through her as she thought of all the years they'd lost. But she knew if she gave in to those thoughts, it would suck her under so she did what she'd been doing for years. She tucked everything away and ignored her sadness for the moment. (Her therapist would be shaking her head, giving her that "you're smarter than that" look right about now.)

Her phone buzzed, making her jump. Her dad again. She rejected the call.

Ezra didn't say anything thankfully.

Not long after that, Lucas called. Then her mom, wanting to assure her that Lucas was studying. Then Mari, Charles, Henri, and then to her surprise Jesse Lennox. He wanted to tell her he'd spoken personally to the architect she was hoping to get on board with her team, and the woman had been wanting to work in New Orleans for ages. It was a really positive update and something he could have simply emailed her. Which told her how much he or Hailey must like Ezra.

Also not surprising, since the man was wonderful. And for some annoying reason he seemed to be fighting his attraction to her. She couldn't figure out why either. Last night she'd seen that look, had understood exactly what it meant.

He still wanted her and she wanted him. No problem, right? *Gah!*

When he suddenly put the SUV into drive, she glanced over in surprise. "We're leaving?"

"You sound way too happy about that." His tone was dry. "And yes, we're calling it. Berlin planted two small cameras so we've got a way to keep an eye on this place."

"Clearly I would make a terrible private investigator because I didn't even see her."

"She planted one when you were on the phone with Mari, when she was posing as a jogger. And the other she went in through the backyard of the neighbor so neither of us would have seen her."

"I'm impressed. So...I want to go have dinner with my mom and Lucas tonight. I know he's safe at my parents' but I miss him. And I think my mom needs to spend time with me." The truth was, she wanted to spend time with her mom too. They'd always been close, and the last couple days had shaken Magnolia's foundation. "You're invited too, but I don't expect you to come."

"I'll come." He said it all casually, topping it off with a shrug.

"You don't have to."

"I'm not letting you out of my sight." His words were a growl, making her entire body...clench.

It was as if all of her muscles tightened at his protective, growly tone, because how could she not be affected? She didn't even trust her voice at this point, so she simply nodded.

And tried to figure out how to convince this wonderful man that he needed to spend tonight in her bed. Simultaneously she wondered if sex had changed in the *years* since she'd had it and if maybe she was biting off more than she could chew.

But then she replayed his words in her head, that possessive tone that turned her insides to mush, and another rush of heat punched through her. *Screw it.*

She was going to get this man into her bed and keep him there.

CHaPTer 15

You cannot please everybody. You are not a taco.

Magnolia sat at the table out on the lanai with her mom, watching Ezra and Lucas play basketball on the hoop her parents had set up years ago when Lucas showed an interest in playing. Luckily her dad was gone for the evening so she wasn't worried about him showing up and ruining the night.

"So how are you doing? For real?" Her mom curled her legs under her on the outdoor couch as she turned to Magnolia. She had on a sparkly Christmas sweater and little ornament earrings that glittered under the lighting.

It was a crisp evening, the sun already set, and there was a nice bite of cold in the air.

"I'm handling things. Ezra's been amazing. I feel guilty that Lucas isn't with me, but I know he's safe here. So." She shrugged, hoping her mom wouldn't push too much.

"Have the police made any progress?"

"No, but Ezra's company might have. They've more or less launched an investigation into finding Perry."

Her mom's blue eyes narrowed. "I want to wring his neck myself. Pathetic excuse for a man."

Magnolia nodded, her reserves of energy depleted. She was angry at Perry, but she was also mentally exhausted and just wanted to be home. Wanted all this to be done with, ending with Perry in jail for a good long time. Being with Ezra was... Well, it was nice, even if the circumstances were garbage. But she felt like her safe space had been taken away from her.

She smiled when Lucas made a long shot, started prancing around like a peacock. Maybe sports was going to be the language these two spoke. She certainly hoped so. It was like the orange ball came out and these two just started acting like they'd known each other forever. She snapped a few covert pictures of the two of them, smiled as she looked at one of Ezra laughing.

"I know that look," her mom murmured.

"Mom, I love you, but I don't want to have this conversation."

"What conversation?"

"About my life choices or whatever. I'm not asking for any sort of advice."

"All I was going to say is that I recognize that look because you had the same one seventeen years ago when you talked about that man right there. I was going to say I think you should 'shoot your shot' or whatever the kids are saying these days."

"Shoot my shot?"

"Yep. I heard Lucas say it on the phone to someone." She nodded imperiously, a grin tugging at her mouth.

"Well nothing is happening. We're just navigating this whole thing and he's keeping us safe. That's it. Nothing more." Magnolia had seen the guard when they'd pulled up, and her mom had told her that she'd invited Scarlett inside last night so she'd be more comfortable. Of course she had.

"Uh huh."

"So how are you doing? With dad?" Dinner had been fairly neutral territory but now that it was just the two of them, she wanted to know.

"Madder than I've ever been in my life." Sighing, she set her wine down on the side table. "I just don't understand what he was thinking. It's such a betrayal."

Yeah, that about summed it up. "He's been calling me."

"He told me. And I told him he needed to stop, to give you room to breathe.

Of course he's not listening," she grumbled.

"Has Lucas said anything to you about him? Or anything, I guess?"

Her mom shrugged, but there was a hint of something in her eyes.

"What?"

"I don't know, I think he's got a girlfriend or something."

"Why?"

"I heard him on the phone last night. Or this morning. I got up to pee because of course I did and thought I heard something. It was about three in the morning. He was in his room on the phone laughing about something. Maybe it was a friend, but..." She shrugged.

"When did my baby grow up?" Magnolia murmured, looking back at the two of them. Ezra scored and was looking quite smug with himself until Lucas stole the ball. "I'm a little bummed he didn't try out for the team this year." Magnolia had loved going to his games, cheering him on.

"Oh, me too. But you were smart not to push him."

Lucas had been playing basketball since he was five and loved it. He'd tried other sports but that was the one he always came back to. He'd been MVP last year as well. So it had been a surprise to everyone when he'd decided not to try out this year. He'd told her that he still loved it, but school ball had become so competitive and was taking up too much of his time. Time he wanted to spend doing other things, he'd said.

His grades were excellent and he still played ball with his friends and tutored kids at the same community center she had at his age so she'd let it go. At first she'd thought it might be something deeper, but he'd just made the decision to do it for fun and on his terms. She could definitely understand that. "He's a lot smarter than I was at his age."

Her mom snorted softly and leaned her head on Magnolia's shoulder. "He has a very good mother."

"Well that's true." She laughed lightly, then waved at the two of them when they looked over. "I think it might be time to call it. Lucas has that test tomorrow and I've got an early meeting."

Her mom sat up. "You're going into the office?"

"Yes. I'll have a bodyguard, just like Lucas." Scarlett would be taking him to school, and he'd be checking in with her once he got there because yes, she was feeling neurotic and worried about him right now. How could she not?

"Oh, I'm sure that man wants to guard all of your body."

She snorted out a surprised laugh. "Mom!"

Her mom just shrugged, but grinned and stood. "All right, Lucas! I know you're almost grown, but you need to shower then get some sleep because you've got a big test tomorrow."

She stood with her mom, just grinning when Lucas looked at her. "Hey, she's the boss." She kissed him on the cheek, went to hug him but he pulled back.

"Ugh, I'm gross."

She didn't care, but nodded. "You know the deal about tomorrow."

"I know, I know. I'll text you once I get to school, then once my exam is done. I'll be with Scarlett the badass the whole time."

"Okay. I love you."

"Love you too." He fist-bumped Ezra, then said he'd text him, which surprised but pleased Magnolia.

Ezra was polite to her mom, but to her surprise, and definitely his, she pulled him into a hug.

"I'm sorry about my husband. I know I don't need to apologize for someone else. But I don't think I gave you a chance when you were younger, and maybe if I had—"

"You're right, you don't need to apologize for him," Ezra murmured, his voice gravelly. "Thank you for dinner Abigail, it was delicious."

Her mom sighed, but then pulled Magnolia into another hug. "I'll text you when Lucas leaves for school in the morning."

"You're the best." She kissed her mom on the cheek too, then headed toward the privacy gate on the side of the house and out to Ezra's SUV.

Only to find her dad pulling into the driveway. "Great," she muttered. "Just get in the SUV, I'll handle him." At least he wasn't blocking them.

Ezra simply looked at her, his expression hard, though she knew it wasn't directed at her. "How about you get in the vehicle and I'll handle him?"

His tone was mild, but she wasn't fooled. *Nope.*

She walked to the front of her father's idling car. Instead of pulling up the rest of the driveway into the garage, he'd parked next to Ezra's vehicle so she knew he wanted to talk.

Might as well get this over with.

"Can we talk in private?" he asked as he got out of his car.

He looked as if he'd aged ten years, which, fine, made her feel guilty. But she pushed it down because she hadn't done anything wrong. He'd made his choices.

"No. I love you, but I don't even want to talk at all right now. I've been ignoring your calls for a reason and you weren't supposed to be home for another hour."

His cheeks flushed and she knew this had been intentional. "I'm sorry. I know I screwed up, but—"

"No, Dad! No buts. Your apology can't have a qualifier." She was aware of Ezra standing behind her, could only imagine his expression. "Your apology also can't only be to me. It has to be to Ezra and Lucas as well. And it has to be real. You have to actually mean it! Because I can't even begin to think about forgiving you if you're not sorry. And I know you're not because you don't think you did anything wrong. You lied to me, to Lucas essentially, and stole his father from him. You stole years from Ezra. From *me*. Years!" Tears burned the back of her eyes and she turned away, knowing the dam was about to break.

She hurried past Ezra and slid into the passenger seat, slamming the door harder than she'd meant to. But it felt good. She wanted to slam all the doors right now. She tried to dash away the wetness on her cheeks, but the tears kept coming.

She was aware of Ezra talking to her dad as she opened the console looking for tissues. Nothing!

Ezra got in the SUV a few moments later, his expression dark as he reversed out of the driveway. "I'm sorry you had to talk to him tonight," he murmured as they left, his voice tight.

She just nodded, because she didn't trust her voice. Couldn't talk at all as the stupid tears decided to fall.

"Hell," Ezra growled and before she realized what he was doing, he'd pulled into the parking lot of a small dog park, parked, then hurried around to the back, popped the hatch. He came back with a roll of paper towels. "They're not tissues, but they clean up blood better."

She snort-laughed at his words, not sure if he was being serious. "I'm sorry," she rasped out through the tears that simply wouldn't stop.

"You have nothing to be sorry for. I'm surprised this didn't happen sooner." He wiped away her tears, then pulled her into an awkward hug.

The center console was too big, and in their way, but she didn't care. She hugged him right back.

Aaannd then crawled right into his lap, straddling him. She'd worn a fitted sweater tonight with a long skirt and belt that was more for aesthetics than anything else.

Ezra watched her, that dark glint in his eyes she recognized oh so well. He wasn't going to reject her tonight. She'd bet her whole house.

"Magnolia," he growled out in that intoxicating whiskey voice. A warning?

She wasn't sure and didn't care. In that moment she felt like that seventeen-year-old who only wanted one thing. Ezra Hunt. Forget consequences or the outside world.

She rolled her hips as she settled down on him, glad she'd worn a long skirt tonight.

He sucked in a breath as she moved over him, his erection sliding right over her unfortunately covered clit. So she did it again, dragging in a hard breath of her own at the sensual contact. A little scrap of fabric and his pants weren't doing anything to hide his reaction to her or the sensation of that thick length rubbing against her. She wasn't sure if she should be embarrassed or not, but so didn't care.

If they continued doing just this, she was going to come from the friction alone.

"We shouldn't..." He trailed off, his eyes going a little glassy when she reached between their legs, palmed his covered erection.

"We'll stop if you say stop," she murmured, feeling empowered being on top of him like this. Sort of in control. Because she very much wanted him, had never stopped. Chemistry had never been a problem for them, and now that they were back in the same location it was like picking up where they'd left off. They couldn't, she knew that, but logic wasn't part of the equation right now.

Instead of stopping, like she'd half expected, he reached between their bodies, under her skirt and cupped her mound with a sort of possessiveness she felt all the way to her core. Her inner walls tightened at the bold move, a flood of heat rushing between her thighs.

"I don't want to stop anything," he growled, claiming her mouth with his right as he shoved her panties to the side, started strumming her clit with determination.

Oh god. Just like that, he started teasing her, rubbing that sweet spot in tight little circles. With his free hand, he held on to the back of her head as he kissed her. Claimed her mouth with an urgency that mirrored her own.

Time seemed to slip away as he continued teasing her, as she relearned the way he kissed, the feel of his body underneath her fingertips. Even with his jacket and shirt on, she wanted to touch him everywhere.

As he slipped two fingers inside her, she gasped. Then he started thrusting them in short little bursts, not nearly enough to take the edge off for what she was feeling, but he felt amazing. She was slick and knew she could come soon, but she wanted all of him.

She grasped onto his belt, managed to get it free as she pulled back in the tight space.

Suddenly the seat eased back, the little whir of the lever moving the seat. "I've got this." His voice was as unsteady as she felt as he managed to shove his pants and boxers down.

She barely had enough time to savor the sight of him after so long before she slid down on him, groaned.

"We need...condom," he growled out even as he thrust up, completely filling her.

She moaned in pure pleasure as he hit her deep, hitting that sweet spot that was guaranteed to push her over the edge. "On...pill," she rasped out as he slid through her slickness again. Because they weren't stopping. *Oh god, please don't want to stop.*

He growled again, the word or words unintelligible, but he didn't seem concerned about protection anymore as he began thrusting inside her.

She met him stroke for stroke, the constricting space adding to the intimacy as they lost themselves in each other in long, hard strokes. Every time he thrust upward, he hit that spot. And every time, pleasure punched out to all her nerve endings.

He was now cupping one breast under her sweater and bra, teasing her hard nipple with sharp little rolls, but she felt the sensation of him everywhere. Both her nipples were hard points, the other one rubbing against her bra in time with his teasing.

"I'm close," she moaned against him.

He thrust upward again, his thick length completely filling her, and she let go. Her orgasm punched through her as pleasure built and built then crested with so much intensity, she came with her entire body.

He came with her, the heat of him coating her as he grabbed onto her hips, still pumping inside her as she came down from her high.

As she finally collapsed on him, he slid his callused hands up her thighs and over her ass, the sensation sending another ripple of awareness and pleasure through her. Her inner walls tightened on his half-hard length, making him groan against her neck. As he held her in place, right on top of him.

"Pretty sure this is how we did it the first time," he murmured.

She laughed, her walls tightening around him again.

He half laughed, half groaned as he eased his hips back. "We've got to get out of here, but we are definitely not done tonight."

She nipped his earlobe, bit down once. "Let's see how fast you can get back to the safe house."

CHAPTER 16

Adalyn swiveled slightly on the bar top stool of the kitchen island, looked at Gumbo who had a tiara on her head and a boa around her neck. "I can't tell if she's plotting to poop in my shoes later or not."

Antonia snickered as she sat next to her, set a cafecito in front of her. "You sure you want this so late?" she asked as she took a sip of her own.

"Yeah, I can sleep anywhere, anytime." And she had.

"Gumbo is definitely plotting something, but she really does look like she's holding court," Antonia said, laughing lightly. "And you were smart to bring her, but now my girls are going to be begging for a dog even harder."

"They've got a bunch at the shelter if you're looking."

Antonia sighed, turned away slightly from the adorable sight. "I hate saying no to anything right now but I can't imagine adding another living thing to take care of at the moment."

Oh, right. "Of course not. Do you need help with anything? And I'm sorry, I know that's a dumb question. But...I want to help."

"Other than the envelopes of cash you left?" The woman's lips quirked up slightly.

Adalyn shifted uncomfortably in her chair. "I thought I was doing the right thing."

Antonia shrugged, glanced back at her girls. An animated movie was on in the background, and the three of them plus Gumbo had now moved onto big throw pillows as they all stretched out. "It's certainly not going to hurt. And I am appreciative. And...if I'm being honest, I invited you here to size you up a little. I didn't think there was a real possibility that Rory cheated—"

"Jeez, no. Never. And I hadn't even seen him in years until everything happened, but no way. When he talked about you and his girls, his entire face lit up like a kid on Christmas morning."

Tears filled Antonia's dark eyes, but she quickly dashed them away. "I know that. In my heart I do. And I knew the risks of his job, but when he made detective, I thought..." She shook her head, glanced away again, looking at the girls. "They're doing well at least. Cara has taken it the hardest, but she's the oldest."

"I'm sorry." Adalyn didn't know what else to say.

"Thank you. We have good days and bad days. My parents are coming to stay for the Christmas holiday so I'll have help while the girls are off school and they'll get to spend time with their grandparents."

"I could...watch them?"

"That sounds like a question."

"Well, I don't know if you should trust me. I don't know much about kids. I feel like Gumbo would probably do a better job than me." Though her husband would probably be perfect. The man was good with everyone, including kids. He just had that personality, that innate goodness about him.

"Do you want kids? I hope that's okay to ask," she added, rubbing a hand over her face. "I know I'm not supposed to ask that normally but I'm pretty sure you and I are past all that."

"Yeah, I don't care and I honestly don't know. Rowan and I have talked about it and don't want any right now. But...maybe. I just want to make sure it's the right time."

Antonia smiled and it softened all her edges. "I don't know if it's ever truly the right time. That said, we waited a few years and I'm so glad we did. I got a lot of good time with Rory." There was a wistful note in her voice and Adalyn could see the exhaustion creeping in.

She slid off the stool. "I'm going to clean up your kitchen then head out."

"You don't have to."

"I know, but I want to. And I'm glad you ordered me to come to dinner tonight."

Antonia grinned, took a sip of her cafecito. "Fleur told me that bossy would work with you. And that you wouldn't say no to tacos."

"My sister is rarely wrong."

CHAPTER 17

Sometimes I want to go back in time and punch myself in the face.

Ezra knew he should have had more control last night in the SUV. Then again back at the safe house—two more times.

And now this morning.

But Magnolia was stretched out against him, all long limbs and soft, naked breasts. Her breathing was steady, but he had a feeling she wouldn't mind him waking her up...

Easing back, he slid down her body, buried his face between her legs and slowly began teasing between her folds and against her clit.

She arched languidly, digging her heels into his back as she spread wider for him. "This is a great way to wake up," she said around a yawn. Then she jolted when he gently sucked on her clit.

He wanted to wake her up every morning like this. Or with some version of this. But that was a pipe dream. Something he knew wasn't part of their future, but he could take right now at least. They'd already talked about birth control after that first time in the SUV and they were both clean. It had apparently been a very long time for both of them, something that shouldn't make him so happy.

But that primal part of him was doing cartwheels because he didn't want anyone touching her but him. Ever. He just wasn't sure how to keep things casual, just between the two of them.

When she squeezed her thighs around his head, her moans getting louder and more urgent, he shelved all thoughts of the future and other bullshit as he brought her to release.

She tasted as sweet as the sounds she made, and when she dug her fingers into his hair, clutched onto his head, he knew she was close. It didn't take anything at all before she was coming against his mouth, her entire body trembling as he stroked her clit through her release.

"Inside me," she murmured, her voice thick with sleep or desire, or maybe both as she reached for him.

When he went to wipe his mouth, she simply tugged him to her, kissing him with a bold, raw sensuality as she spread her legs to accommodate him.

She was so wet that he slid right inside her tight body. She sucked in a breath, just as she had last night as she adjusted to his size, but pleasure and lust filled her gaze as he began moving inside her.

And god she was tight, clenching around him so hard he had to concentrate on his control.

He moved slowly at first, as he took his time kissing along her jaw, nipping her earlobes, stroking her breasts. He wanted to touch her everywhere, kiss and suck and lose himself in her as they both found release.

The second he felt the change in her body, the quickening of her inner walls around his length, he knew she was close. He began thrusting harder, deeper, savoring the way she dug her fingernails into his ass and back as he slammed into her.

She met him stroke for stroke, her second orgasm of the morning hitting faster than he'd anticipated. So he let go of his last shred of control, coming inside her with a possessive growl as he nipped her neck, knowing he'd likely leave a mark.

In that moment he didn't care at all because he wanted the world to know she was off-limits.

"That's a lot better than coffee," she murmured, stroking her fingers up and down his back in an intoxicating rhythm. Her touch was soft, gentle, damn near hypnotizing.

"No kidding." Groaning, he eased out of her, resisted the urge to rub his release onto her thighs because he wasn't that much of a caveman. Okay, he definitely was, but he needed to show some control.

"Ugh, I need to shower and get ready but I wish we could stay here all day." Sighing, she shoved the tangled covers out of the way and stood.

Little beams of sunlight peeked in through the roman shades, more than enough for him to see all of her.

He groaned as well, swung his legs over the side of the bed when all he wanted to do was pull her back to him, bury himself inside her again. "I'll grab you coffee while you're in the shower." He cleared his throat, tried to find the right words. "Listen...uh, I don't think we should...necessarily tell Lucas about this or anything."

Standing in the entry of the half-open bathroom door, sunlight bathing her in a golden light, she froze. "What?"

"I just don't think we need to tell him or make this like..." *Damn it.* He struggled to find the right words. "I just want to make it clear that..." He cleared his throat again, realizing his mistake as she stared at him, her blue eyes hurt. He was mucking this all up really, really nice.

"Well, he wasn't on my list of people to call this morning, Ezra," she snapped. "And you're right, we won't make this a thing. This was just a one—or two—day thing. We'll just call this what it is, sex." Then she stepped into the bathroom and shut the door behind her with a resounding click.

"Magnolia—"

He heard the lock on the bathroom door, then the shower start, and he froze. She was locking him out. Rightfully so.

And what the hell was he going to say anyway? There was no good way to say they should keep things casual and easy, especially when it was the opposite of what he wanted. He wanted to marry her right then and there, had always wanted that.

But that was insanity talking.

Grabbing his clothes, he dressed and hurried back to his own room. He didn't want to lose the scent of her on him, but he showered anyway because he needed to be back in control. Needed to keep his head on straight. He'd been a fool to think they could just do casual sex.

Nothing between them had ever been casual, and throwing sex into the mix now was like throwing accelerant on an already raging bonfire.

CHAPTER 18

Magnolia answered emails on her tablet as Ezra drove to her office. A small, petty part of her had considered getting into the back seat but she'd quickly shelved that. That wasn't who she was, and she wanted to handle this like an adult.

Unfortunately she wasn't even sure what there was to handle. Maybe acknowledge that they wouldn't be having sex again? Because she wasn't sneaking around and hiding something from anyone. But clearly Ezra didn't want anything else from her.

Which fine, fair. Even if it cut right to the bone.

She just wished he'd told her before they'd done anything, not directly after she was basking in that wonderful post-orgasm feeling. "You can pull in there. I'll tell you the code."

She nodded to the gated parking lot next to her office. Off-street parking was considered prime in New Orleans so they guarded their lot vigilantly like everyone else.

As he steered into the parking lot, she turned off her tablet, sighed. "Look, I don't want any weirdness between us. Not now. Things clearly got out of hand last night...and this morning. But you're right. We'll just keep things friendly from now on. No messy stuff." AKA sex.

He was silent as he pulled into her marked parking spot. Then he turned to her. "I messed up this morning—"

"No, you were right. I wish your timing had been a little better." Her tone was dry. "But if we start doing, well, whatever, it could get messy. And you're just getting to know Lucas and I don't want anything to screw that up. So let's chalk last night up to a sort of reunion. And now it's over and we'll just be adults. We'll be friends." She nodded once, proud of herself. They could do this.

Ezra sort of grunted, then got out of the SUV, was around the front before she'd even unstrapped. He had her door open and plucked up her purse before she could. "So what's on the agenda today?" he asked, glancing around, definitely looking for a threat.

He already knew how many cameras were here—Berlin had told her that she'd hacked into them, was monitoring them. Which made her think they needed to get a whole new system, or maybe a security upgrade, but that was something for future Magnolia to deal with. But at least she knew that Berlin was keeping an eye out and felt a whole lot safer since no one seemed to be able to find Samuel Perry.

"I've got a Zoom meeting with Mr. Lennox's contact, Tabitha Johnson." He'd told her to call him Jesse, but it felt a bit weird. "And..." She trailed off, frowning.

"What?" Ezra's entire body tightened and he looked ready to spring into action. Today he'd worn dark slacks, a button-down white shirt and a custom jacket that was hiding a pistol and probably other weapons. He looked delicious in the suit, but it did nothing to hide the warrior beneath the civilized clothing. The man with the whiskey voice and amber eyes who'd stolen her heart long ago.

The man she was going to be "just friends" with now. *So great.*

"That SUV belongs to a man named Austin Jameson. He's my competitor for this job. He's been vying for Tremblay to come on board with his team as well. His company is strictly construction. Jameson Construction. And they're good, but he's...a lot to deal with." Rude, pompous, entitled, misogynistic. The kind of man who needed a good punch in the throat.

Jameson had gotten a few contracts her company had wanted and vice versa, but he had a personal beef with her. One she didn't even want to think about. Secretly she thought he hated that her company was so diversified, that they weren't solely a construction company.

She ran a niche type of company, something no one else in the state did. They owned a couple boutique hotels, worked with job placement for women who needed it, and personally oversaw very specific construction jobs. Some were new, and some were restorative. She was very particular about those types of jobs because she and her team had to bring on contractors, to create a team from scratch. And she didn't always use the same contractors, whereas most construction companies around here tended to use the same contractors. Or they pulled from the same pool.

And she realized she'd fallen into that trap by trying to snag Tremblay. *Huh.* She was annoyed with herself, but moved past it because today she was making changes.

"What's that look?" Ezra asked, sliding his hand to the small of her back as they walked toward the entry door.

She swiped her card, waited for the flash of green to open. "I just had a realization that I've been working on this bid all wrong." She'd been trying to play by someone else's rules. As she headed down the hallway toward the bank of glass-windowed offices and open space where they set up various plans, she smiled at her assistant, Kendra.

"Hey, look who just dropped by," Kendra murmured, giving a subtle eye roll in Jameson's direction before she handed Magnolia a binder. "These were just dropped off and you've got that Zoom meeting in twenty minutes, but I know you haven't forgotten that. I hope we get to work with her," Kendra whispered, her gaze straying to Ezra curiously.

"This is Ezra, my...associate. He's going to be working with me today." She kept it vague, knowing Kendra wouldn't question her either way.

"Magnolia." Jameson's voice was loud, grating on her very last nerve as he turned away from Charles's open office door. "Finally showing up to work, I see."

Beside her Ezra stiffened. Keeping her fake smile in place, she half turned to Kendra. "Will you show Ezra to my office?"

She knew Ezra was a professional, but a dark energy was rolling off him and she wasn't sure how he'd react against the biggest asshole on the planet. She turned back to Jameson, keeping that smile in place she knew made him crazy. "What are you doing here?"

He sauntered—yes, sauntered—through the open area of their office as if he owned the place. His gaze strayed to a set of plans they had on display but the job was mostly done and not a secret. "Just stopped by to say no hard feelings about us snagging Tremblay. I know he's been yanking us both around." Even when he tried to sound sincere, his tone was just douchey.

"No worries at all. We've already moved on with someone more innovative."

He blinked in surprise, his gaze narrowing ever so slightly. "Who?" he demanded, what little veneer of civility he had slipping away.

"You'll find out soon enough." She wasn't worried about losing Tabitha Johnson to him, but still, she was playing this one close to the vest. Kendra was the only one she'd told about Tabitha and she'd marked the meeting private on the calendar. "Good luck with the bid," she added. "I'll walk you out." Without waiting for his response, she headed for the side door, assuming he'd follow.

She was well aware that everyone else was quietly listening from their offices, but no one would peek out and ask questions until he was gone.

"I haven't heard of any other architects going up against Tremblay for this bid."

"It's because I'm using someone from out of town. Recommended personally by Jesse Lennox," she added because fine, apparently she was a little smug about this and wanted to rub it in Jameson's face.

His expression went blank for a moment, maybe from surprise. "I didn't know your father was friends with Lennox," he said, not even trying to be a jerk, she was certain. He was simply *sure* that she couldn't have made the contact herself. Because that was who Jameson was. *Ugh.*

"My father doesn't know Lennox. I do. We met on a different project since he's been buying real estate in New Orleans. He really loves it here and wanted to help me out." Mostly true, and the real estate purchases weren't secret at all. Some of her friends and associates had been speculating about why he was buying up real estate.

Jameson simply grunted, but already had his cell phone out as he exited the building. Smiling to herself, she headed back down the hallway to find Charles leaning against Kendra's desk.

"Hey, sorry about him." He rolled his eyes. "He showed up when I was just arriving. I couldn't think of a good reason to tell him to wait outside. He just wanted to rub it in about Tremblay."

She laughed lightly. "It's fine, he's all bluster anyway. And he can have Tremblay because I'm working on something better. I'll let everyone know the details at our one o'clock meeting." She glanced at her cell. "And, I've got a meeting."

She found Ezra in her office standing at one of the big windows overlooking a huge magnolia tree. "Hey, sorry about that."

He turned, his expression carefully neutral. "Is there a chance that asshole has been the one targeting you, not Perry?"

She blinked in surprise as she set her bag on her desk. "What?"

"Kendra told me the two of you dated."

"We did not date. And I don't have time for this," she snapped. "I appreciate you coming with me today, but I need a clear head for this Zoom call."

Oh, he definitely wanted to argue with her, but he quietly stalked from the room. And not in the way that jackass had basically stomped down the hallway. No, Ezra moved like a predator, was whisper quiet as he shut the door behind him.

Shaking off thoughts of Jameson and everything else, she sat down and turned her laptop on. It was time to do this.

CHAPTER 19

Ezra moved to the lobby, a small glassed-in area away from the main set of offices and Kendra's desk. There was an admin behind a simple desk who'd offered him a beverage while he waited.

He'd declined but was now calling Berlin as he sat in the plush area surrounded by glass. Outside, oak and magnolia trees shaded the entire area, making this place feel a lot bigger than it actually was. The furniture blended with the outdoors, with creams and dark browns, and the metals were all a bronze coloring. There were a dozen smaller plants indoors as well that were clearly kept up and watered, including a lemon tree.

There was a small bookshelf with newer books, magazines, and no television in sight. But soft classical music pumped in from speakers he couldn't see. The whole environment was meant to put people at ease.

"Everything okay? I'm watching you through one of the exterior cameras. I wish she had them inside so I could hear everything."

He turned toward the bank of windows, wondered which camera she was watching him from. "A man named Austin Jameson stopped by. He's the competitor for her current bid and a real asshole." And Ezra could admit he was pissed that she'd basically shunted him to her office when she was talking to Jameson. "And apparently they used to date." Maybe. "I want you to do a deep dive on the guy, see what you can find." He kept his voice pitched low so the admin wouldn't overhear him. She was busily chirping to someone on the phone so he didn't think she was paying attention to him anyway.

"Oh, Jameson, I recognize that name. Big construction company. And I'm on it," she murmured. "Anything else?"

"Nope, not for now. I'm sure you'd tell me, but any news on Perry?"

"No, and I kinda wonder if the guy is dead. Or just not in town because it's hard to totally disappear."

Hard, but not impossible. "Okay, thanks." As he set his phone down, it buzzed and Skye's name appeared on-screen. One of the founders of Redemption Harbor Security and an all-around badass. "Hey, everything good?"

"Yep, of course. Just checking in."

Okay, Skye never just checked in. Not with him anyway. He glanced over at the admin desk area, saw the woman working on her computer intently. Strolling to the window, he looked out at people passing on the street. Mostly joggers and a few moms or dads out with strollers, everyone bundled up to some degree. Magnolia's building was in a mostly residential area, but there were a few other non-homes he'd seen on the way, including a lawyer's office and a bed and breakfast. Her building blended well with the environment, something he was certain was intentional. "Everything is good enough here. Still trying to find the threat." He kept it vague in case the admin could hear him.

"How are things with you and your son?"

Ooooh, so she was just dropping that. "Good, I think. We've been texting." Which was a little surreal, but he found he liked it. At least it made it easier to think about what he was going to say. "And we played basketball together last night." Something he'd enjoyed more than he would admit to anyone. It had been... Hell, he didn't even know how to put it in words.

"Okay, just checking. Rowan and Adalyn have been pretty tight-lipped about things and I didn't know if maybe there was an issue."

He smiled because of course those two were keeping things quiet, even with their boss. "No issue." Other than himself. He'd screwed up this morning, and now that Magnolia was all *we'll be friends*, he wanted to drag her back to bed so she completely removed the word friend from her vocabulary.

He really was screwed up.

"I've got Berlin looking into something else, another potential issue." He glanced at the admin through the reflection, was glad to see she wasn't paying any attention to him at all.

"Good." She started to say something else, but there was a shout of concern from beyond the waiting area.

"Gotta go." Without waiting, he rushed past the desk into the area of main offices and saw Magnolia on the ground, her face turning red as she clawed at her throat. His entire world tilted on its axis. *No. No, no, no.*

Kendra and Charles were crouched next to her, looking horrified and useless.

"EpiPen!" he shouted as he raced toward her.

She pointed with a shaky hand, her other still clutching her throat.

Ignoring everyone who was just standing around making worried sounds, he sprinted to her office, dumped out her bag, snatched up both EpiPens that fell out.

Back in the center area, he shoved her cousin out of the way, uncapped the pen and slammed it into her thigh. He uncapped the other, waiting to see if the first didn't kick in fast enough.

But she sucked in a breath, tears rolling down her cheeks as she struggled to sit up. He slid his arm under her back and helped her sit up.

"Kendra, get her two bottles of water now. Charles, call 911. Now!" He looked between the two of them before focusing on Magnolia, who was still dragging in lungfuls of air.

"Do you need the other pen?" he asked.

"No...I'm okay," she rasped out, still breathing hard.

He rubbed her back in small circles as Kendra dropped back down, her fingers trembling as she tried to uncap the first bottle. He took over and opened it, holding it steady for Magnolia to sip.

After a few sips, she took it in her hands.

"Do you know what happened? Only answer if you can talk. And everyone go back to your offices!" he ordered as he turned to look at the cluster of people. "She doesn't need you staring at her." He knew he sounded like a dick. Didn't care.

Magnolia gave him a ghost of a smile as her employees scampered away. "It happened so fast. I ate... I just took a nibble of one of the brownies in the break room. I'm only allergic to—"

"Mushrooms, I remember," he murmured. "You, sit with her," he ordered Kendra, not caring that he was taking over. "I'll be right back." Uncaring what the hell anyone thought, he gently kissed Magnolia's forehead, then got up.

He made his way to the break room, saw a handful of various snacks in the middle of a table. They all had plastic coverings, including a tin of brownies which were part of a huge gift basket. He pulled out his cell phone as he rummaged around in one of the drawers for a gallon plastic bag. Just something that he could use to preserve this.

"Flores here."

"It's Ezra. I'm at Magnolia's office and I believe someone tried to poison her. She had an allergic reaction to brownies, the only thing she ate this morning. And her only known allergy is mushrooms. I don't know if this is related to what's going on, but I don't believe in coincidence."

"I don't either. I'm on my way. Is she okay? Have you called 911?"

"Yes, she's okay because she had an EpiPen, and yes, the cops are on the way. I'm securing the brownies now."

"Good. I'll see you soon."

Kendra stepped into the room, her dark eyes wide. "She's okay but—"

"Do you know if she drank anything else this morning? Coffee, water?"

The woman blinked. "Ah...yeah, water." She pointed to the fridge. "She always uses the filtered water, pours it into a travel bottle."

He nodded. "Okay. No one comes into this room at all and no one leaves. Go spread the word."

Eyes still wide, she nodded and he finished bagging up the brownies, held on to them as he hurried back into the main area.

Magnolia was now sitting at Kendra's desk, working on her second bottle of water. And to his surprise, the rest of the office had listened to him, mostly. People were standing in doorways of their offices, worriedly watching, but no one was crowding her.

He crouched down as he set the bagged brownies on the desk. "Camila is on her way as well as the police. And I know you're going to argue, but I think you should go to the ER or at least the walk-in, get your blood tested."

She looked at the bagged brownies, understanding dawning in her pretty blue eyes, then back at him. "You think this was intentional?" she whispered.

"I don't know. But I don't think you should take any chances."

"Okay," she whispered. "I'll go."

If someone had poisoned her, that someone was going to pay dearly.

CHaPTer 20

*I try to take one day at a time, but sometimes
several days attack me at once.*

Pacing in the hallway outside Magnolia's hospital room, Ezra held his cell up to his ear. "What do you mean it's gone?"

"I don't know another way to say it, Ezra," Berlin said. "There's no freaking footage and it's not that it was erased. The security cameras were turned off sometime around eight o'clock this morning."

"I thought you hacked the system."

She sighed, very clearly annoyed with him. "I did. And from about eight thirty onward, I have a record of everything on my end. But I can't recover something that was never recorded."

He bit back a curse, curbed his temper. This wasn't her fault, and if there was something to be found, Berlin would find it. "You're right, I'm sorry—"

"You don't have to apologize. Of course you're worried."

"Is there any way to—"

"To find out who was in the office at the time the security was turned off? Yes. According to the keycards used, almost everyone, which sucks for us. Only two people got in around eight thirty so they're off the list of potentials who messed with security, but not off the list completely."

As two nurses in scrubs rushed down the hallway, he backed up against the wall. "What about Austin Jameson?" he murmured.

"I can't know when he arrived for sure, but the side door opened from the inside about eight fifteen. I have no way of knowing if it was him, but no one else used their card so it had to be someone letting him in. And without recordings, I have no idea if he's even the one who brought the brownies."

Ezra had only been able to ask Kendra and Charles about the food before heading to the hospital with Magnolia, and neither of them remembered if someone had brought the brownies in separately or if they'd been part of the giant gift basket they'd received from a client last week.

"I'm cross-referencing some traffic cameras to see if I can nail down when Jameson arrived. If I can find out his VIN—which I'm still working on—I'll just hack his vehicle and get his records that way."

"Thank you." Once they disconnected, he tucked his phone away, worried that they'd been looking at this situation all wrong.

It was possible Samuel Perry had somehow broken in to her place, but given his track record Ezra didn't think he was that smart. And how would he have known about her allergy?

Mulling over what he knew so far, he stepped back into the room just as Magnolia's doctor was finishing up. Magnolia's expression was tense, but her doctor simply nodded and left.

"What's wrong...other than the obvious?" he asked, stepping forward as she picked up her purse.

"I just got a call from Lucas's school. He's been called to the principal's office for fighting and might be suspended."

CHapTer 21

*Not everything that weighs you down is
yours to carry.*

"Lucas is a good kid," Ezra murmured as he steered into the parking lot Magnolia directed him to. "I'm sure there's an explanation."

The high school looked more like a college campus. The school buildings were all red brick with pristine lawns, the American flag and Louisiana state flags whipping proudly in the wind at the entrance.

"I know. I can't even imagine what this is about." Her entire body vibrated with energy as he pulled into a parking spot, her hand already on the handle before he'd fully stopped.

"Listen, I need to ask something before we go in. Is there a chance that Anderson knew about your allergy?"

Still tense, she paused, her fingers wrapped around the handle. "He...actually does know about it. We went to a gala together years ago. I can't imagine he actually remembers, but yeah, I did tell him about my allergy. He was all weird about people with allergies, saying they were mostly made up. It's the only reason I told him about mine, to shut him up. And I can't think about him right now." She jumped from the vehicle before he could say another word.

He followed after her, quiet as she signed the two of them in and made polite small talk with the admin at the front desk. The woman was behind a plastic barrier in an open office area and it was clear Magnolia knew her.

A door next to the admin's area opened and Lucas strode out, hands shoved in his pockets. He looked surprised to see Ezra, but just glanced down instead of making eye contact with his mom.

A man in a suit and tie stepped out, his expression neutral enough. "Let's talk first," he said to Magnolia with familiarity, then continued. "Then I'll talk to both of you together," he said, looking at Lucas. He flicked a curious gaze at Ezra, but didn't say anything more as Magnolia headed inside.

"You want to get some fresh air?" Ezra asked.

Lucas nodded, looking relieved as they headed out into the brisk sunlight.

Ezra nodded toward a couple stone benches. "Want to sit?"

Lucas shrugged, but sat, crossed his arms over his chest.

"Want to talk about it?"

Another shrug. "Not much to say. I punched a guy and he deserved it."

"How about you tell me the whole story?" Because Ezra couldn't imagine Lucas just punching someone out of the blue. He might not have known him for long, but the kid had a good head on his shoulders.

Lucas sighed, some of the steam leaving his body. "Some asshole, a senior I used to play basketball with, was showing off a...picture of a girl from my class. I don't even know if it was real but he was laughing and showing everyone in the locker room, saying nasty things about her."

"Was she dressed in this picture?"

Jaw tight, Lucas shook his head.

"How old is she?"

"I dunno. Sixteen, I guess. Maybe fifteen. I took his phone and smashed it. Then he took a swing at me so I punched him. And I'm not sorry about what I did. I don't care if I get suspended!"

Ezra ran a hand over his face. "When you go back in there, I'm going with you. Just don't say you're not sorry. Let me do the talking. Do you have the cell phone?"

He shook his head. "The principal confiscated it. It's in his desk. I saw him put it there."

"Okay, come on." As they walked back into the building, Magnolia was stepping out of the principal's office, her expression pinched as she moved toward the two of them.

"I think we're going to be able to work this out with a short suspension," she murmured.

Ezra frowned. "He's not going to be suspended."

Now she frowned, but the principal motioned for them to come inside. Ezra followed, ignoring the surprised look, and held out his hand instead.

"I'm Ezra, Lucas's father. I've been out of the country but I'm back now."

The man looked shocked as he glanced at Magnolia for confirmation.

"We're not able to talk about his job," she said cryptically, her smile neutral.

Ezra smothered a smile, mainly because he was pissed about this morning and now this bullshit. His kid wasn't getting in trouble for doing the right thing. *Nope.*

"Okay then...let's discuss this. I've talked to Conway's parents and they want this to be handled quietly as well. I think a few days of in-school suspension and extra community service for both boys will do. And it won't go on their permanent records. Conway is already accepted into college and he's sorry about what he did."

"He's sorry he was showing off naked pictures of a minor?" Ezra asked as he sat next to Magnolia in one of the little chairs in front of the gigantic desk.

Magnolia gasped.

He glanced at her, frowned. "You didn't know?"

"I thought they were fighting in the locker room over a girl," she said, looking stunned. "Just shoving each other." She turned that ice-blue glare on the principal, her entire demeanor changing. "Now what's this about pictures? Is this about a girl here at school? And why aren't the girl's parents involved? Is she okay?" she demanded.

The principal cleared his throat nervously.

"That phone is evidence so I hope you haven't done anything to it," Ezra said before the man could respond. He'd learned that overwhelming a target with information could be a very effective tactic. "I've already reached out to Detective Flores about this situation." A little lie but one he could back up later if necessary. "In my profession, I work closely with law enforcement," he said, leaning closer. "And it's concerning that our son has been brought in here with threats of suspension when he was simply trying to stop one of his classmates from distributing inappropriate, likely illegal material. I'm not sure if the other individual involved is eighteen—"

"He is," Lucas murmured from the seat behind them.

"Ah, well that definitely changes things." Ezra sat back, trying not to look smug. "We'll be involving the police immediately."

CHAPTER 22

I wish I was full of tacos instead of emotions.

Magnolia was still reeling from everything today and it was only one in the afternoon. She turned around in the front passenger seat to look at Lucas, who was on his phone as Ezra steered out of the parking lot.

"Did you at least get to take your final?" she asked. After being in the hospital, then the tense meeting with the principal, she simply wanted to sleep but that would come later.

Grinning, he nodded. "Aced it. That was awesome how you went at him like that," he said, looking at Ezra, who was quietly driving.

Ezra simply lifted a shoulder. He'd been all calm about everything when she'd wanted to strangle the principal's neck. That sneaky bastard. All he'd been concerned with was making sure nothing was made public, that the two boys from wealthy families didn't face any blowback. And very likely he didn't want the school to receive blowback. He hadn't said *one* word to her about the young woman involved when she'd talked to him privately. He'd made it sound like two boys had simply gotten into a scuffle over a girl, but that everyone wanted to let it go since it was the holiday season. He'd made it sound like he was doing them a favor with a short suspension. Jerk was trying to cover his ass and the school's ass.

Then he'd tried to backtrack in the office and say the only reason he hadn't said anything about the young woman involved was that he couldn't talk about a minor, but that was bullshit.

"Just so you know, Martina just texted me, said she's headed down to the school with her mom. She's on scholarship and I think that's why Principal Merrick was trying to sweep this under the rug. Plus Conway's parents donated a bunch of money to the solarium project."

"Asshole," she muttered. She didn't care for the Beauregard family and this only added to it.

Lucas looked at her in surprise, likely because she'd probably cursed in front of him only one or two times in his life, then grinned. "Yep. She said her mom reached out to Camila after I gave her the detective's number. Camila is going to meet them there to confiscate the phone and take her statement."

"Good." Magnolia nodded through her exhaustion. Getting potentially poisoned this morning then being called to her son's school had not been on her bingo card this morning. "So...are you dating this girl?" she asked, hoping she sounded casual.

Lucas blinked. "No. And I don't need to be dating someone or into them to do the right thing for them. What he was doing was wrong. Gross."

"I know," she said, reaching back and squeezing his knee. "And I'm so proud of you."

He nodded, then frowned when he saw the little ID bracelet on her wrist. Crap, she'd forgotten to cut it off in the rush to get to the school. "Wait, what's this? Were you at the hospital today?"

"Yes, but everything is fine. I had a bad reaction to mushrooms. Luckily Ezra was quick with the EpiPen and everything is totally fine." She pulled her sweater sleeve down, silently cursing her mistake.

"You're really careful about what you eat."

"We think it was in some brownies, and intentional. The cops have sent the food to be tested," Ezra murmured.

Magnolia knew that Ezra had also kept one brownie and tucked it away so his team could get it tested faster. She glared at him. "Really?"

"He has a right to know." And Ezra sounded totally unapologetic about it.

Oooh, her feelings toward him were so complicated right now. She was grateful he'd taken over at the school today—and you know, saved her life!—but he was still maddening.

"I do have a right to know," Lucas said from the back, indignant.

"Of course you do. I'm just exhausted," she said, leaning back against the headrest. "And I won't be talking about this anymore." Sniffing, she closed her eyes and tried to tune everything out.

Her son was okay, not suspended, and now that Camila was involved, Magnolia knew she would handle the legal end of things. She also knew that the school mess likely wasn't over and that there might be more fallout, but she couldn't do anything about the situation now.

And if she was being honest with herself, she simply wanted to crash for a couple hours and block out the entire world.

"Your mom is okay," Ezra continued. "And I'll make sure nothing happens to her."

Lucas sighed but she heard him mumble "Okay."

She turned in her seat. "I really am proud of you. Truly. It's hard to stand up to stuff sometimes, especially when others don't agree with you."

He lifted a shoulder. "I had a good teacher."

She reached back, squeezed his knee once more before she sat back and closed her eyes again.

CHAPTER 23

I'm going to start yelling plot twist every time something goes wrong in my life.

Magnolia stumbled into the safe house kitchen, still exhausted after her hours-long nap, but she'd forced herself to get up. She wanted to eat something, check on Lucas—who'd surprised her by wanting to stay at her parents again—and then catch up with some emails at work and make sure everyone knew she was okay. Maybe she'd wait for the emails tomorrow, she thought, scrubbing a hand over her face. It was nine o'clock and she could get some more sleep after food.

As she rummaged in the fridge, Ezra and Berlin stepped into the kitchen.

"Hey," she murmured, smiling at both of them.

"Sit, I'll get you something." He expertly moved her out of the way and she was too tired to argue.

And why would she? She was exhausted. If he wanted to feed her, she was so okay with that. "Do you have anything in the Italian family with lots of carbs and red sauce?"

He snickered slightly. "Yeah, but it's all old. I'm going to order you something."

Berlin cleared her throat loudly. "I'm hungry too."

Ezra looked up, sighed. "When are you not?"

She cleared her throat again, her expression pointed.

"Fine, when are you not, *oh wise one*?"

Magnolia blinked, looked between the two of them. "What's happening right now?"

"He lost a bet, said I couldn't hack...ah, said I couldn't do something, and I did. And now he has to call me 'oh wise one' at least seven times in a row, in front of other people."

Magnolia snickered. "He really should have known better."

Berlin grinned. "I knew I liked you."

Magnolia glanced down at her phone as it buzzed, scanning another email from one of her employees. As she started to exit her email app, a new message popped up.

From an unknown sender with the message *Too Bad*. Even before she clicked on it, her stomach tightened.

Too bad you survived. Next time you won't be so lucky. Attached was a picture of her being rolled out on a gurney (because Ezra had insisted) with an X over her face.

Her phone clattered to the countertop, her fingers icy and numb.

"What..." Berlin snatched up her phone, cursed, then raced from the room.

"What just happened?" Ezra demanded.

"Someone emailed me a threat and a picture of me being rolled out of my office today. Whoever wants to harm me was watching and waiting for the fallout. I want to go pick up Lucas now," she blurted, shoving her stool back.

"We will," he murmured, rounding the island and pulling her into a tight embrace.

She buried her face against his neck, dug her fingers into his back and held tight. "You think Berlin will find him?" she mumbled against his face.

"If anyone can, it's her. Come on." He eased back, but didn't remove his hand from the small of her back.

She savored the feel of his fingers against her body, even with her sweater. She didn't care if they were just friends now—he grounded her, and more than anything, she needed that right now.

As they headed for the garage, he glanced at his cell phone, then gave her a look she couldn't read.

"Oh god, what is it? Did she find him?"

"Your mom texted your phone. Berlin told me to tell you...she says to get over there right now and to hurry. No one's hurt," he added.

Okay, if no one was hurt, she could deal with this. "Let's go."

Luckily they didn't have far to go, but Magnolia was crawling out of her skin the entire short drive. She'd texted Berlin back, told her to text her mom that she was on the way. She'd really wanted to call Berlin and ask for an update but knew she'd just slow the woman down.

As Ezra pulled into the driveway, she was surprised to find Lucas already there, arms crossed over his chest as he leaned against the back of the SUV Ezra had loaned to him. They hadn't wanted him driving his Jeep around. He straightened when Ezra's headlights flashed over him and Magnolia was out of her seat before he'd even turned off the ignition.

"Are you okay?" She raced at Lucas, looking for any visible signs of injury.

"I'm fine, Mom." He just sounded frustrated and a hint of anger was in his amber-colored eyes. In that moment she could see more of Ezra in him, the man he was becoming.

"What happened?"

"I—"

The front door opened and her father stalked out, her mother behind him. All the Christmas lights were on, but the cheery backdrop was a sharp contrast to the dark expression on her dad's face. Her mom just looked...sad.

Ugh. What the hell was going on?

"I caught Lucas trying to sneak out," her father ground out as he approached. Even though it was later, he was wearing slacks and a polo shirt.

She glanced at Lucas, and to her surprise, her son stuck his chin out defiantly. But he didn't respond one way or another.

Sighing, she squeezed his arm. Her kid had been through a lot today and shown what an incredible person he was by standing up for someone who couldn't stand up for themselves. It would have been easier for him to say nothing, but instead he'd put himself out there. "You're coming with me. Will you go pack all your stuff?"

"I've already packed. My bag's in the SUV," he murmured.

"Okay, I love you and we'll worry about whatever this is later."

"Are you just going to let him get away with this?" her father demanded, stalking toward them.

Magnolia had never seen him like this, so angry. She knew that anger and fear came from the same place, but at this moment she didn't care. Because she could not deal with one more thing today. "Get in the SUV and just wait," she murmured. "You'll follow us."

"I'm not going to deal with this right now, Dad. Lucas is coming with us and we'll talk about this later." She didn't miss how Ezra moved up beside her, took a little step forward so he was technically in front of her.

Protecting her.

And her heart simply squeezed. He'd always been like that.

"Lucas has never been so disrespectful before. And now that man is back in his life, he's acting out, sneaking out!"

Oh, no. She reached out, placed a hand on Ezra's forearm when she felt him tense. "Dad, Lucas is a great kid. He's understandably upset right now, and no, I have no idea why he was sneaking out. I'll talk to him later since I'm his mother. Considering he's a straight-A student who's never given me a hint of trouble, a kid who has more courage than I did at his age, I'm going to wait to rush to judgment. And you have absolutely no right to put any of this on Ezra, a man you literally stole from."

Her father made a scoffing sound.

"You stole time from him! You stole his time as a father! You stole from me," she shouted again, feeling her own anger rise up in a tidal wave that had a red haze over her vision. Looked like keeping all that stuff buried wasn't healthy. She'd be sure to tell her therapist how right she was later. "I'll never know what we could have had and neither will he. And Lucas will never know what it was like to have

Ezra as a father during his most formative years. So you don't get to say one damn word about how Lucas is acting." She looked at her mom, who had tears in her eyes.

And right now that was her only sadness, that her mom was stuck in the middle.

"I love you, Mom. I'll text you when we get back to the safe house. Unless you want to come with us?"

Her mom shook her head, but then her father opened his mouth to say something. She'd never know what because Ezra stalked forward, nearly stepping completely in front of her.

"Don't." There was a lot of anger in Ezra's voice as he zeroed in on her father. It was tempered, but it was there, a low growl. "Whatever you're going to say to her, don't. Most people don't like to think they're the villain in their own story, but right now you should do some soul-searching before you say something you'll never be able to take back." Then he turned back to Lucas, who hadn't gotten in his vehicle and instead stood and watched everything with wide eyes. "Your mom will be driving you back and I'll follow you both."

Nodding, Lucas handed Magnolia the keys and she got into the driver's seat, still shaking, but she managed to pull it together and reverse as soon as Ezra did.

"I should have insisted you come to the safe house with me, I'm sorry," she said as she pulled onto the familiar street of the home she'd grown up in. Of the one Lucas had spent his first five years in. God, what would their life have looked like if her father hadn't mucked everything up?

"Don't apologize, Mom. I wanted to stay with Nana. And I kind of thought you and Ezra might want some alone time."

She shot him a surprised glance, but quickly looked back at the road, cleared her throat. "Ah, we're not in the safe house alone. A handful of Ezra's friends, coworkers I guess you could say, are there too. And we're not... We're friends."

"Whatever you say," he murmured. "And I'm sorry for sneaking out. I've been keeping something from you. Not because I didn't trust your reaction but...I don't know. I have a girlfriend and she was performing at a local theater tonight. I wanted to catch her show, but with everything going on, I figured you'd say no."

"Because it's not safe. Someone poisoned me today." And had sent her a nasty follow-up message.

He shoved out a breath. "I know, I just wanted to see her."

Oh god, he sounded miserable. "Okay, well, you're not in trouble." Maybe that was crappy parenting, but she was going with her instincts. "But I need you to understand how serious this threat is. I'm questioning myself right now, thinking we should get out of the city, but..." She shook her head as she pulled up to a red light. "For the time being, the safe house is probably the most secure place we could be. Other than your grandparents'," she muttered even as she tried to shove her anger back down. "Though considering you were sneaking out, maybe it's not so secure."

"One of the sensors on the window needs a new battery. I, uh, told Nana to just silence that sensor until I replaced it. I also might have taken the battery out."

"Oh, Lucas." She shouldn't laugh, she *shouldn't*. But a snicker bubbled up and it turned into an almost maniacal laugh. "It's not funny, I've just had a very long day and I've clearly lost my mind."

"It was the second floor," he added. "I figured no one was breaking in that high. A thief would try one of the lower ones if they were going to try anything. I didn't plan on Grandpa being outside smoking a cigar." He paused. "I've never seen you yell at him like that."

"I've never yelled at him before." *What a mess.*

"I'm glad you said all that to him."

She sighed, turned on her blinker at the stop sign. People were out looking at Christmas lights and slowing them down when she just wanted to get back to the safe house. "I probably shouldn't have shouted at him."

"He deserved it. And you were right, he *did* steal, from all of us. And I don't think he expected, like, the fallout, or whatever. I bet he thought he was doing the right thing, but it's still wrong and he shouldn't just get to move on like he did nothing wrong."

"Very true. I just hate that Nana is caught in the middle."

"Yeah, me too," he muttered. Then his eyes lit up as she pulled down the driveway of the big home. "This place is sweet."

"Yeah, it's pretty nice. Have you eaten yet?"

"A while ago, but I could definitely eat again."

She continued down the driveway, pulling around to the back where there was a whole area for parking out of sight from the street. "So, this girlfriend..."

Lucas cleared his throat and shrugged. "Her name's Emma. I met her at the community center. She goes to a different school. She's a senior and doing dual enrollment with the community college. She's really into theater and so freaking smart."

"A senior, huh? An older woman." She waggled her eyebrows.

"Oh my god, *Mom*!" He looked at her with horror. "I'm almost seventeen. And she's just seventeen."

And there was the kid she knew. She grinned, the weight that had been pressing on her chest almost all day easing up just a fraction. "I'm just messing with you. Mostly. Because I'm definitely going to want to meet her. When you're ready," she added when he gave her that look again. "But sooner than later."

"Yeah, okay."

"And no more sneaking out."

"Moooom." Again with the long, drawn-out word.

Ezra was at her door, opening it and effectively cutting off the girlfriend conversation. But that was okay. She slid out and wrapped her arms around him. She knew she'd surprised him, could feel it in his tentative grip, but she didn't care as she buried her face against his chest. "I just needed a hug." Her words were smothered.

But he heard her because he said, "Anytime you want."

Suddenly she thought of something and jerked her head up. "Where's Scarlett? I thought she was watching him."

"She was taking a dinner break," Ezra murmured. "Which your mom knew about so I'm guessing Lucas did too." He shot a glance over as Lucas rounded the vehicle.

"Ah…yeah. I knew my window was small and I'd planned to leave my phone at the house," he muttered. "So you guys wouldn't know I was gone. I figured if she saw me sneaking back in, I'd just take my punishment."

Magnolia blinked at her son. "I'm a little worried that you've thought this out so well."

Lucas lifted a shoulder, his expression sheepish. "Can we grab some food and talk about my punishment later? I'm starving."

Of course he was. "I already told you I'm not punishing you. I figure your good deeds from today and the crap show going on right now evens everything out," she murmured as they followed Ezra to the back entrance of the house. "You're getting this one on the house."

"I'll take it."

Ezra simply shook his head as he ushered them into the kitchen.

Berlin was waiting for them, her expression dark. "I found the asshole who sent that message."

CHAPTER 24

"What's the word, B?" Ezra asked Berlin over his earpiece. Normally that was what they called Bradford, but he wasn't here for this op and they were sticking to initials for this one.

"According to the police scanner, there's a pileup on I-10 and a robbery at a brewery that's taking up everyone's time. In addition to the normal Monday night bullshit. There are two cars dedicated to your area but they've both been pulled into the pileup. It's a bad one unfortunately. But you're all clear for the next half hour at least. And that's even if a neighbor calls the cops, which I'm not betting on."

"Thanks." He looked at the others in the SUV—Tiago, Adalyn and Rowan—all wearing balaclavas. "We good to go?"

Rowan nodded first. "Let's do this."

They'd parked in front of an abandoned house that had a crumbling *FOR SALE* sign and no signs of life. It was two houses down from their target house in a struggling neighborhood that had never recovered from the last hurricane. Maybe it would eventually, but for now, none of the streetlights even worked and at least three of the homes were known drug houses.

Including the one where the threatening email to Magnolia had come from. It had only been forty-five minutes since he'd left her and Lucas back at the safe house and he had to stop thinking about them, to focus on the job at hand.

To find Samuel Perry—and not kill him. Probably.

"You got eyes on the drone camera, B?" Tiago asked. "I'm putting my tablet down." He'd flown one of their smaller drones to get a full aerial view of the one-story dumpster fire of a house. The backyard had three rusted bikes piled in one corner, a washing machine, two dryers and at least three tires stacked up against the back fence. He'd set the drone down on a tree branch with a solid angle on the front door.

"Yep. No one coming in or out of the front door or any of the side windows on the east side."

The direction they'd be infiltrating.

"Let's do this," Adalyn murmured. "If we can't meet back here, go to the secondary meetup point."

They all nodded their agreements and slid out of the SUV. There might be eyes on them but Ezra didn't get that tingling feeling he normally did when being watched. Moving down the sidewalk in a single formation, they fanned out in the small front yard, with him rushing down the east side of the house, only stopping when he reached the edge of the back wall.

Weapon up, he peered around. He could see the camera on the back porch, but it was pointing in the opposite direction. "I'm taking out the camera," he murmured as he hoisted himself up on the high porch from the east side.

"I'm at the front door, out of view of the camera here," Tiago said just as quietly.

"By the west side window." This from Adalyn. "I can see a naked woman sleeping, the TV on mute, through a crack in the blinds, but nothing else."

"There's no one in the window on the east side." Rowan.

"Everyone, gas masks on," Ezra said quietly as he reached around from behind and taped over the camera. Then he slid off his balaclava, shoved it in one of his pockets, then slid his gas mask on—and pulled out his flash-bang.

"Three, two, go." He kicked in the back door, tossed his flash-bang, heard glass breaking, knew the others were making their entrances as well.

Shock and awe were sometimes the best option. Hell, more often than most.

Pistol up, he moved into the house on silent feet, sweeping into what turned out to be a kitchen.

A man in a white tank top and jeans staggered up from the table, crashed into the refrigerator.

Ezra moved fast, went to take him down, but out of the corner of his eye, saw movement. *Hell.*

He ducked at the incoming blow, twisted to the side and landed a punch in the other attacker's gut.

The guy grazed Ezra's head with his fist, but was too off-balance from the blast and smoke. Ezra moved behind him, kicked him hard so that he flew into his buddy.

They crashed to the floor, destroying a rickety table with it.

A screaming mostly naked woman ran past the kitchen and out the back door.

Gunshots sounded in the front of the house, but he had to tune it out for now. His team knew how to take care of themselves.

Ignoring the fleeing woman, he pinned the guy closest to him on the ground, slapped zip ties on his wrists and ankles. Just as he finished, the second guy was on his feet, a SIG in his hand as he stumbled at him.

He managed to get off a shot before Ezra returned fire, hit him once in the upper thigh. The guy screamed and tried to swing around, shoot him again, but Ezra had him down and on his stomach in seconds.

Flex-cuffs on, he stood, kicking away the weapon before he scooped it up. Normally he'd have aimed for the chest, but they wanted anyone here alive to answer questions.

Neither of the men he'd just restrained were Perry—he had that guy's face memorized. But the guy who'd shot at him was Danny Murphy. An all-around piece of shit with a long criminal history who was also friends with Perry. "Clear in the kitchen," he spoke quietly, ignoring the cursing and moaning from the two men.

"Front's clear." Tiago. "One tango down."

"I let the woman get away. And I'm clear." From Adalyn.

"I took down one too," said Rowan. "Don't recognize him from our file."

"Stay where you are, then. I've got Murphy in the kitchen. B, you see anything on the drone?"

"No movement in the neighborhood that I can see and nothing on the police scanner. No one's called anything in yet." Clipped, precise words.

He might miss working with Hailey, who'd been their hacker for years, but Berlin was a total pro and knew her shit.

He rolled Murphy over, kicked him in the hip when he tried to lash out at him with his bound legs. "Nope. You're going to answer some questions or I'm going to shoot you in the face."

"Eat shit!" the guy snarled, his grungy beard needing a good wash. Or maybe a shave, considering bits of food were caught in it.

"Not if you were the last being on earth." Ezra stood, stalked to the refrigerator while keeping his eyes on both men.

The other one was staying very still, likely hoping Ezra would forget about him.

Ezra opened the fridge, started shaking condiment bottles, found rolls of cash in two of them. Then he opened the freezer, found stacks of cash hidden behind frozen beef. He began setting the cash on the table, then grinned when he found a handful of diamonds in a salt shaker in one of the cabinets.

"Well, well, well, look what we have here." Ezra held them in his gloved hand, was pretty sure they were real. "I didn't expect this."

"I'll kill you!"

"Yeah, yeah, I've heard it before. Now, if you want to get out of this alive, you're going to tell me everything I want to know about Samuel Perry."

Even shot, bleeding and clearly in pain, Murphy frowned up at him. The smoke had now cleared from the room and his pain receptors were likely kicking into high gear, but he was surprised. "What? Why?"

"Because that asshole has pissed off my boss." He made a big show of touching his ear so it was clear he was talking to someone else. He didn't need to touch his earpieces, but didn't want to explain shit to this guy. "Clean out the rest of the house. Weapons, cash, jewels if you find them."

"Boss? Who the hell do you work for?"

Ignoring the question, he crouched down next to Murphy, placed his pistol over the guy's crotch. They were running low on time in case someone decided to call the cops in, or worse, more of this guy's crew showed up—which was a possibility since that woman had left. She'd had a little time to call for help. "Where is Perry? And don't lie to me. I know he was here tonight."

The guy swallowed hard, his eyes flicking down to the pistol without moving his head at all. "He was here, just grabbing some stuff he left behind. I told him he couldn't stash his shit here anymore, that's all!"

Ezra pressed his weapon harder against the guy's crotch.

"I swear! Some detective was hassling me yesterday about Perry, demanding to know where he was. Something to do with his bitch ex. I don't know, I swear!"

"You keep swearing, but I don't believe you." Ezra's voice was low and calm.

"He's telling the truth." The other man said from on the opposite side of the destroyed kitchen table. "Perry came by here to get his stuff, then left."

"Did he say where he was going?" Ezra didn't take his eyes off Murphy.

"Nah, just said he found another place to crash."

"I found the phone he used to text M," Adalyn said through the earpiece. "Looks like he texted his ex too. Lots of nasty messages, all threats about how he's going to make her pay for leaving him."

"Whose phone did he use earlier?" Ezra asked.

"Phone?" Murphy stared up at him dumbly.

"Yes, phone. Your boy was texting someone."

"He's not my boy!"

"Yet you let him store his stuff here." Ezra cocked his head to the side slightly.

"Yeah, because he's a psycho! And...I owed him. He got me out of a jam a few years ago but now we're square."

"This is just a standard burner," Adalyn said again. "He could have got it here or just left it when he was done."

Damn it. "Where do you think he might have gone?"

"Ah...I don't know."

Ezra pressed down on him again. "Think *really* hard."

"There's an SUV moving down the street, driving really slowly. Might be time to get out," Berlin said. "You've got maybe three minutes."

Adalyn strode into the kitchen then, so covered up that no one would ever be able to make out even her hair color. Hell, maybe not even that she was a woman. Silently, she scooped up the cash and diamonds and dumped them into a garbage bag she'd found who knew where.

"We're slipping out a side window. We'll meet you in the backyard," Tiago said. "Hurry."

The guys in the kitchen wouldn't even see them, wouldn't know their build.

Murphy shifted underneath him, sweat pouring off his forehead as he tried to back away—but there was nowhere for him to go. "Um...there's this chick he sometimes crashes with. On Fourth Ave. I don't know the street number, but that's it, I swear! You don't have to take my stuff."

"You can tell your bosses that this is courtesy of Samuel Perry. That bastard stole from my boss, so we're taking back what he took." A complete lie, but it wouldn't hurt to have more people gunning for Perry. And this robbery muddied the waters of why they were really here. He couldn't let anyone know that this was related to Magnolia because it could make her a target.

Hell, this might be the best way to get that rat out of hiding.

Ezra stood then, keeping his weapon up and trained on the two men as he raced out the back door.

"They're at the house." Berlin's voice was tight. "Three guys. I think someone called them. Maybe from a neighboring house. Or the woman who escaped."

"I'm at the back fence," he murmured as he used the washing machine to jump over it with ease. He raced across another overgrown backyard and met the others on the neighboring street.

"Come on," Adalyn ordered, and the three of them fell in line behind her. There were a few people on their front porches smoking, but no one said anything to them—even with them wearing freaking gas masks. When they reached the next street, they made a hard left then looped back to the street they'd just come from.

"I think we've got enough time," Adalyn said quietly as she replaced her gas mask with her balaclava.

Standing in the shadows of a giant oak tree dripping in old Mardi Gras beads, they all did the same.

"Let's go," she continued.

Knowing it was a risk, they raced back to their SUV, sticking to the shadows along the sidewalk. As they reached their vehicle, Ezra could see someone coming out of Murphy's stash house.

"Gun it, I'll take out their SUV." He was already rolling down his window, had his pistol out and aimed as Rowan gunned the engine, drove right past the house they'd just robbed.

Murphy was on the front porch, shouting at someone, but dove for cover when they squealed by.

Ezra aimed, fired, *pop, pop*, took out the back tires.

Their shouts faded as Rowan took a sharp right, gunned it again.

"I'll direct you using the fastest route," Berlin said over their comms. "I can see those losers on the feed. They're not going anywhere," she practically cackled.

Ezra leaned back as relief slid through him. He wasn't sure tonight had been useful, but it sure hadn't hurt. And they were going to destroy the drugs they'd found and donate all the cash.

Their normal M.O.

"Berlin," he started.

"I've already begun a search on anyone linked to Perry who lives on Fourth Ave."

He grinned, even with a tightness in his chest. He wanted Magnolia safe and Perry gone. "You're a rockstar...oh wise one."

She snickered over the line. "You know it."

CHAPTER 25

Never let anyone treat you like regular glue.
You're glitter glue, baby.

Magnolia opened her eyes when she felt Ezra's bed shift, realized his hair was already wet...and he wasn't wearing a shirt.

Ooooh. She hadn't even heard him get back in but he'd clearly already showered and changed into jogging pants to sleep.

"Hey," she rasped out, still swimming in that in-between place of sleep and not quite dreaming as she shifted against his bedcovers. "Everything okay?"

"Yeah," he murmured, sliding under the covers and moving right up next to her.

"I'm not here for...whatever. I was just worried." She tried to sit up slightly, but he stretched out and pulled her onto his chest. Oh, okay, she really liked that. Maybe she actually *was* dreaming? "I didn't think you'd be gone so long and I guess I fell asleep."

"We ended up driving around after our op, then ditched the SUV and commandeered a new one."

"Commandeered sounds a lot like steal."

"Sort of."

He let out a sigh and that was when she realized it was raining outside, could hear the little patter of light drops against the window and roof. Fairly rare for

December, but the sound was soothing. "Do you care if I stay? I don't want to be alone after today." She thought she'd been keeping her shit together pretty well, but the day's events had taken a mental toll on her. At least she knew their son was safe under this roof.

"Of course you can." He wrapped his arms around her, pulled her closer.

She was basically splayed across his chest, and whew, he was even more built than she remembered. But with more scars unfortunately. She traced her finger over one she knew wasn't from his service but from his father, human garbage that the man was. A long slide along his rib cage where his father had "just been showing you how a switchblade worked." Ezra had been twelve at the time.

"Can you tell me about tonight?" she asked, when it was clear he wasn't going to just spill everything.

"We didn't find Perry, but might have a lead."

"That's pretty vague. Care to share any details?"

"I'm not trying to keep you in the dark intentionally. I just...don't want you to know this side of what we do."

Frowning at the odd note in his voice, she leaned up, looked at him, some of her sleep fading away. "Why not?"

His amber-colored eyes were clear enough with the moonlight streaming in from one of the windows. "This isn't the kind of stuff..." He cleared his throat. "I just don't."

"I don't need your protection from stuff. I'm a big girl. A *woman*."

"I know you're a woman." His gaze fell to her mouth, hot and hungry. But he didn't make a move. "Maybe I just don't want you to know all the details for my own sake."

Sighing, because she was pretty sure that was all she was getting from him, she laid her head back on his chest, nuzzled into him. Then she grinned to herself at the way he sucked in a breath. "Just give me a few details."

"We found the phone Perry used to text you. He texted his ex-wife too."

"Yeah, I talked to her. She said he's been sending her nasty messages. She's gotten a new phone, one she uses for work and just life, but she's been keeping her old one to keep track of his texts as proof if...well, just if."

"He wasn't at the place where we found it, but we gathered some information from the people there."

"Where is there?"

Another sigh, but at least he answered. "A drug house. We cleaned them out." And he sounded absolutely smug about that.

She snickered. "Can't really get mad about that. Who are they going to call, the cops?"

He laughed lightly too. "We disposed of the drugs, and we're going to anonymously donate the cash we took. I suggested the centers that you work with."

She stilled her finger on one of his scars and resisted the urge to look up at him. Because if she did, she was going to kiss him. Or attempt to, and she didn't feel like getting rejected tonight. "That's really kind, thank you."

He shifted slightly under her, likely shrugging. "How's Lucas?"

"Good, I think. We watched a movie, then he went to his room early when his girlfriend called." She did look up at Ezra then. "It's weird knowing he has a girlfriend. I have so many questions but I'm trying to give him space since he's dealing with so much right now."

"It's probably better not knowing some stuff." His tone was dry.

She laughed lightly. "No kidding." Closing her eyes, she curled up with him, telling herself she could keep things easy between them.

But she knew she was lying. She was already attached, had been for a long time. And she'd never gotten closure either, just lost the man she'd loved, wondering why he'd ghosted her. Then she'd found out he hadn't at all. Now here she was in bed, unfortunately clothed, with the man who was the epitome of her fantasies.

And he just wanted to stay friends.

Thanks a lot, universe.

"What?" he murmured, lazily stroking his fingers down her back.

Oops, had she said that out loud? "Nothing. Just dozing off and mumbling to myself."

He kissed the top of her head. "Get some sleep."

Yeah, like that was happening now. But she murmured something that sounded like "You too" and just…lay there on top of him, too many things running through her mind until her brain finally had enough.

And she fell into a dreamless, hard sleep.

***

Magnolia opened her eyes and found herself plastered on Ezra's chest. Since she (a) had morning breath and (b) still wanted to jump him, she oh so quietly eased out from his hold and ducked out of the room before he could wake up.

Of course the universe decided to laugh at her because her son was stepping out of his room, which was on the other side of Ezra, right as she clicked Ezra's door shut.

Lucas blinked once. Twice. Then he grinned. "Morning."

"This isn't what it looks like…not that I have anything to be ashamed of if it was. But it's not…and you know what, never mind. How'd you sleep?" Her brain was back to going a hundred miles a minute.

He shrugged, but was still grinning. "Good enough. I'm going to grab breakfast."

"I'll meet you down there in a couple minutes." She needed to brush her teeth and change. And probably run a comb through her hair. And… *Get it together, Magnolia!* Sometimes she hated her brain, hated that she couldn't ever seem to turn it off.

Once she was feeling presentable and had her equilibrium back, she headed downstairs to find almost everyone in the kitchen.

Lucas was sitting next to Berlin, looking at her laptop and speaking a language she didn't understand. Or barely. They were talking about coding and creating a new type of VR game, but that was where her understanding ended.

"There's two of them, apparently." Adalyn gave Lucas and Berlin a pointed look as Magnolia sat next to her at the island.

Ezra gave her another one of those heated looks she felt straight to her core as he made her a mug of coffee. And she knew it was for her because he was doctoring it the way she liked it.

Friends, schmends. She wanted to bang his brains out right now.

Just not right here in front of everyone, because that would be awkward.

Oh wait, Adalyn had said something. Magnolia cleared her throat. "Yeah, I'm glad he understands all that stuff. He's been taking coding classes since he was ten, outside of school. He actually asked to take them so I knew he was serious about it."

"Computer nerds are going to rule the world," Berlin said without looking up.

Lucas fist-bumped her, making Magnolia smile.

She also felt better that he wasn't going to be bored out of his mind stuck in this safe house all day. Because until they figured out where Perry was, she wanted him staying put.

CHapTer 26

"See? Everything went smoothly." Magnolia smiled up at Ezra, who hadn't wanted to let her come into the office this morning.

And if she was being honest, she'd have preferred to stay at the safe house and work from her laptop. But she'd wanted to show everyone at work that she was okay, especially after yesterday.

They'd all been prepping a huge deal and she was the lead. The owner. Everyone needed to feel confident right now. If they didn't get this bid, they'd be fine, but she wanted the challenge of this one. And fine, she wanted to stick it to Austin Jameson.

Maybe she was as petty as him. *Ugh.*

Ezra's expression didn't change as he stood from the seat in front of her desk.

She'd left him in her office while holding a conference call with her team about the architect they'd scored for this bid. And they were *very* excited. Christmas Eve was in one week exactly and they were to have their bids in by the twenty first.

The Gray Corporation planned to go over everything over the holiday break and let everyone know who'd won after New Year's. Then if her team won the bid, it was time to get to work.

And the rest of her meetings had gone smoothly as well. Plus she'd put out a few fires for a handful of other projects. It was good she'd come in, but she was definitely ready to call it a day.

Her desk phone beeped, then Alice, the firm's admin, came over the line. "There's an Austin Jameson at the front desk to see you. I've explained to him that you're in a meeting but he's been insisting—"

"It's fine, Alice, I'll be out in a minute. Don't offer him any refreshments."

"Absolutely not." Magnolia swore she could actually hear the smile in Alice's voice.

"I'm coming with you." Ezra fell in step with her, and while she had no problem dealing with nuisances, she was glad for his presence now.

Going into anaphylactic shock after over a decade of not dealing with an allergic reaction had shocked her system. A server at a restaurant had made a mistake years ago and given her the wrong dish. Luckily she'd had her EpiPen—always did now. She carried it in her purse religiously. After her recent attack, she now had one in her pocket for good measure.

She let the glass door to the main set of offices click behind her before she and Ezra strode across the lobby toward an annoyed-looking Jameson.

He shoved up from the couch he'd been lounging on while angrily typing something into his phone. "Did you tell the cops I poisoned you?"

She blinked in surprise. "Excuse me?"

He took a menacing step toward her, his normally handsome face mottled with rage. "I got pulled out of a meeting by some bitch detective asking if I poisoned you."

She doubted it had happened that way at all. "I have no idea what you're talking about. I do know that the police were planning to question everyone who was here yesterday morning after I went into anaphylactic shock."

Next to her Ezra was quiet, but his presence was a comfort to her.

"Bullshit! You told the cops I poisoned you—"

Ezra moved in front of her when Jameson took a step closer, waaaay too much into her personal space. "You need to leave now and you're officially banned from this building. If you don't comply, we'll be taking out a restraining order against you."

The man turned all his ire on Ezra, who was a lot bigger than him. And a lot more dangerous, though Jameson might not realize that in his agitated state. Or maybe he did, because he took a small step back.

But Magnolia saw it. Internally smirked. *That's right, big tough guy wants to get in my face, but not Ezra's.*

Jameson looked Ezra up and down but didn't say another word. He simply sneered, then swiveled on his heel and stormed out.

"Do you want me to call the police?" Alice was out from behind her desk, eyes wide. "He's always been creepy, but that was scary."

"You don't need to call anyone, but he's not allowed in the building again. Please send out an all-staff message that no one is to allow him inside."

Alice nodded, then turned, her heels clicking quickly as she hurried back to her desk.

She glanced back at Ezra, saw him pocketing his phone with a smug expression. She wanted to ask who he'd been texting, but simply said, "Let's get out of here." She'd done everything she'd needed and anything else she could handle from the safe house.

He just grunted as he placed his hand at the small of her back, using his body to protect hers as they stepped out into the gated parking lot. She wasn't even sure if he was aware of it, but he used his body as a shield, and good god, universe, she was only so strong!

Maybe she could bribe the universe. *Hmmm.*

Once they were in his SUV and pulling out, she said, "So who'd you text back there? Because you looked like the proverbial cat that ate the canary."

"It was nothing," he said a bit too quickly.

"Oh, was it your girlfriend?" she asked, hoping for a reaction.

He shot her a confused look. "I don't have a girlfriend."

"I know." Or, she'd been pretty sure he didn't have one. "So what did you do? Because I know that look. You *did* something."

"I might have asked Berlin to snag the recording of Jameson cursing at you and calling Detective Flores a bitch from your security feeds."

She hadn't been sure what she'd expected, but it hadn't been that. "Why?"

"It's going into a file we have on him. Over the last six years he's had a handful of women quit his company after complaints of sexual harassment. He's currently being sued by two of them. We're saving this and sending it to their lawyers to help their case. The disrespectful way he speaks to you and about a female detective on that recording could help add to the picture they're trying to paint of him. A very accurate picture, I might add. Maybe it'll never make it to court, but it could force him to settle."

Okay, now she was truly surprised. Speechless, at least for a moment. "I've never even heard a whisper about him like that. Sure, he's a jerk. A big one," she admitted.

"One you dated?" he asked as he merged into the heavy traffic.

There was construction on the opposite side of the road—because there was always construction here—so four lanes were now two and the congestion was going to be bad the whole way home.

"Oh my god, we didn't date! I don't know why Kendra said that. We went to *one* gala together and I hadn't even realized it was a date. I thought it was a professional, networking thing—" Her words ended as Ezra cursed.

"Hold on," he ordered.

She jerked forward under a bone-rattling impact as someone slammed into them from behind. They didn't fly into the flow of heavy traffic as Ezra slammed on the brakes. She jerked forward, but the seat belt held firm, holding her in place with bruising force.

"What the hell?" She turned around and realized that this wasn't an accident.

A black pickup truck with a grill on it reversed, then slammed into them again.

Ezra kicked the SUV into reverse, held the wheel tight, the tires squealing as he pushed back against the force of the truck.

"He's trying to push us into traffic!" Oh god. She whipped out her phone, called Camila instead of 911.

"I've got this," Ezra gritted out, his eyes on the rearview as he pressed on the gas. Their tires continued to squeal loudly as he revved it.

Just as suddenly Ezra threw the SUV into drive as the pressure stopped.

The oversized truck swerved onto the sidewalk, then over the grassy, tree-lined median, knocking out an azalea bush as he flew into the opposite direction of traffic.

Horns blasted, and people shouted obscenities, but the guy kept going, shoving his way through cars, knocking little ones out of the way until he ran up on another sidewalk, then took a hard right turn out of sight.

"Magnolia, are you there!"

She realized Camila had answered. "Wh... Yeah. I'm here. We need help."

CHAPTER 27

*This too shall pass. It might pass like a
kidney stone, but it'll pass.*

Still shaken, even hours later, Magnolia slid into the damaged SUV as she and Ezra left the police station behind.

A CCTV camera had caught Perry escaping the scene so at least they knew it was him for sure. Which only made her feel nominally better because the psycho was still out there.

"You're not going to the office anytime soon," Ezra said, his words tight.

She was surprised he'd wanted to keep the SUV but he said it was still drivable and that the company would take care of it. "I know." Sighing, she let her head fall back. It got dark earlier here and they'd been at the police station for hours.

Dusk was settling in on another insane day.

"You're not going to argue with me?" He shot her a surprised look before pulling out of the parking garage.

She was impressed he'd managed to even park the beast in one of the spots. "A lunatic tried to shove us into traffic. Anything that I need to handle can be done via phone or Zoom. I'm not putting myself, or you or anyone else in danger again. I just wish they'd catch him."

"Berlin's currently looking for him. She roped in a friend of hers to help as well."

"He already ditched that truck," she muttered. So she wasn't sure what Berlin could do.

The cops had told them the truck had been ditched less than a mile from their attack. He'd left it in a grocery store parking lot, then from the CCTVs they'd found, he'd headed out on foot, disappearing into a shopping center.

"Have faith, she's good at what she does."

Magnolia just sighed. She didn't trust her voice not to break, so instead of calling, she texted Lucas. *Have you eaten dinner?*

Yep, grabbed some leftovers. I'm crashing early tonight.

She glanced at the time, surprised. But maybe she shouldn't be because she was ready to crash too. He'd been through a lot of emotional turmoil too, and not just having to move to a safe house. His whole world had been turned upside down.

Okay, we'll be home soon. I'll see you in the morning. I love you.

Love you too.

"Lucas is safe at least," she muttered, more to herself than Ezra.

But he reached over, squeezed her hand. "You are too. Perry won't be able to hide much longer, not after the shit show from today. That was stupid on his part, which means he's getting desperate."

"I just heard back from Perry's ex-wife. He sent her a slew of wild texts. She thinks he's either drunk or high. She's currently safe in her hotel room and security is aware of the situation so they're extra vigilant."

"The cops are sitting on the hotel too. He won't get anywhere near her," Ezra said reassuringly.

"I know. I'm just ready for this to be over." How many times had she said that or thought that over the last few days? "I keep thinking if I'd handled things differently—"

"Nope." Ezra shook his head as he pulled onto another crowded street, maneuvering past two arguing bicyclists and a Santa Claus with a beer in his hand. "You don't get to take that on. You handled everything the right way. This guy is violent and angry and there's nothing you could have done to magically change that. Do you think if his ex-wife had done things differently, he'd have not been violent with her?"

"Of course not, Mr. Logic. I was just feeling sorry for myself and stewing."

"You can stew, but don't take on any guilt. I know we've got leftovers at the safe house, but do you want to order anything different?"

"Maybe I can cook. I'm tired of leftovers."

He nodded as he glanced in the rearview mirror, shifted lanes.

"Are we being followed?"

"Only by Scarlett."

She blinked. "Really?"

"Yeah, I asked her to tail us when we left the police station." He glanced down at the incoming text on the SUV's dashboard. "She says we're good. No one attempted to follow."

At least that was something.

***

"Adalyn's going to be so mad she missed this." Berlin sat at the island top, the only other one with them, and dug into her plate. "I didn't even know pesto lasagna rolls were a thing."

Adalyn and Rowan had gone home with Gumbo, and Tiago and Fleur were back at her place so it was just Berlin, Magnolia, and Ezra. And Lucas, who was still up in his room.

"They're Lucas's favorite." Part of the reason she'd made them. And also they were incredibly easy compared to regular lasagna. "And I can teach you how to make it," Magnolia said as she sat next to Berlin, picked up her glass of white wine.

"Or you can just marry me," Berlin said around a mouthful of food.

Ezra knocked into her once before sitting on the other side of Magnolia. "Shut it, B."

"Yeah, yeah." But she sighed happily as she continued eating.

Magnolia turned to Ezra, still reeling from the day, but glad it was a smaller group tonight. She just wished Lucas hadn't gone to bed so early. At least she hadn't had to tell him about what had happened earlier.

"How's your mom doing?" Ezra asked in that deep whiskey voice that reverberated to her core.

"Good enough. Still mad at my dad, still making him sleep in the pool house. She's busy this time of year with her friends and different groups so I think that's helping, but..." She shrugged. "Still trying to figure out what Christmas is going to look like. You know, if we can even go home by then."

"You'll be able to, I'll make sure of it." There was a promise in his voice she took to heart.

"So...if you want to come over for Christmas—like I said, if we can even have it—we'd love to have you. We do a big lunch with friends and family. There might even be flag football in the backyard."

"Ah..." Ezra got this weird look in his eyes.

And it was like a punch to the gut. "Oh, no worries if you can't. No pressure," she added, feeling her face heat up. Clearly they weren't on the same page. "I'm sure you have plans with everyone already but I just wanted to throw it out there. Lucas would love to have you over."

"Is that invite for everyone? Also, will you be cooking this?" Berlin asked, thankfully giving Magnolia a reason to look away from Ezra (and not die of embarrassment from his oh so clear rejection).

Magnolia shoulder-bumped the other woman. "You're definitely invited and I'll cook for you anytime you want. You've done so much for Lucas and me, I don't know if I'll ever be able to thank you."

"I take payments in pasta." Berlin grinned again before polishing off her food. "And I'm about to go for seconds."

Magnolia smiled even around the lump in her throat. Ezra had made it clear that he didn't want anything more than friendship but now she wondered about even that. The man was hot and cold and she couldn't exactly push him about things.

Well, she could, but they were stuck under this roof until further notice and she wasn't going to stir things up with nowhere else to go. Sure, she could get a hotel room for her and Lucas, but she also didn't want to uproot him again.

"That's weird." Leaning against the countertop by the stove, Berlin glanced down at her phone, then looked up. "Ezra, did you open any of the windows...ah crap." She hurried from the kitchen without further explanation.

Ezra moved quickly after her, and since she wasn't hungry anymore, Magnolia did the same even as a sinking sensation settled inside her. It grew as she realized they were headed to Lucas's room on the second floor.

She sucked in a breath when she saw his bed was empty. Oh, he'd tucked a couple pillows underneath the covers, but he was gone. And...she didn't see his cell phone anywhere either.

"Did someone break in here?" Feeling panicked, she whipped out her phone, ready to call Lucas.

But Berlin stopped her. "I'm pretty sure that little shit snuck out. No offense," she added.

"None taken." She'd rather he'd left of his own accord than... Oh god, she couldn't even go there. "What happened?"

Berlin didn't look up from her phone as she spoke. "When I was working on tracking Perry's face through different systems, I think Lucas must have disabled one of the window sensors. Because the activity log is showing that the window in his room," she jerked a thumb behind her, "was opened right after he came up here and said he was crashing. No wonder he was asking me about the placement of all the security cameras." She groaned. "I'm so dumb."

Magnolia pulled up the location app she shared with Lucas and frowned. "He must have turned off his location." Even as she said it, a burst of panic exploded inside her. Taking someone the size of a grown man would be difficult, but what if...

"I've got his location," Ezra said right as Berlin said something similar.

Oh right, they'd added a tracker to both their phones.

Ezra was already moving toward the door. "I've got this, Magnolia. Stay here with Berlin. I need to know you're safe."

She wanted to argue with him—hell, storm out with him—but he was right. "Okay. Just call me as soon as you find him."

She hoped Lucas had simply done something stupid like gone to meet his girlfriend. Not...

No, she couldn't go there. Because something happening to him was unthinkable.

CHaPTer 28

Ezra eyed the neighborhood as he drove down the street. A lot of cars were parked on the street, some in driveways, not much room between houses. Most of the houses were decorated for the holidays and there were enough kids' bikes and toys left in yards or on porches that it was clear this was a family-friendly neighborhood.

He followed the dot that represented Lucas's phone to a little ranch-style home painted a cheery yellow he could only see because of the streetlights. Porch lights were off and there was a teal Celica in the driveway. On the back window was a small sticker that said *support local arts*. Berlin had done a search on Lucas's girlfriend—Magnolia did not know—so he knew that was her car.

He parked behind it, scanned for any potential threats, didn't even see any cameras or security system signs. Instead of infiltrating the house, he decided to just...knock on the front door.

After knocking for a third time, the door flew open and Lucas stood there, looking a little like a deer in headlights, but also a teeny bit defiant. Yeah, the kid wasn't sorry at all.

And Ezra understood, considering how many times Magnolia had snuck out to see him. God, they'd been so reckless back then, but he couldn't muster up any regret.

Lucas glanced past Ezra. "Is my mom with you?"

"No, just me."

Lucas let out a long breath then stepped back. "Is she pissed?"

"She's worried about you," he said as he walked into the cozy home.

A girl with jet-black hair streaked with red and green peeked around a corner, her dark eyes wide.

"You can come out." Lucas held out an arm and a petite young woman about his age darted out from the other room and slid right into his hold. Lucas cleared his throat. "This is Emma, my girlfriend. Her mom split town without paying rent so Emma's friend said she could crash here for the week while they're visiting family in Mobile for the holidays. I didn't want her to stay here alone."

"Normally I sleep at the theater but they had a big thing tonight so I couldn't." Her voice was soft, nervous.

"Well you guys aren't staying here. Go pack up your stuff, both of you."

"I'm not going into the system." Her body language changed, going completely rigid.

"I know. You're both coming with me. We'll stay at the safe house for now. I assume you told her what's going on?" He looked at Lucas, eyebrow raised.

Lucas nodded. "I thought I couldn't tell anyone about the safe house." There was a hint of sarcasm in his voice.

Ezra bit back his exasperation. "Well if you're going to sneak out and put yourself in danger anyway, you're both coming with me. And your mom cooked pesto lasagna rolls."

His eyes widened slightly. "Is there any left?"

"Maybe. I'm not sure if Berlin devoured them all but if you hurry, you might get lucky."

As the two kids went to get their stuff, he texted Magnolia. *He's with his girlfriend. I'm bringing them both back. They're hungry... Maybe go easy on him? We were a lot dumber at his age.*

She just sent him back a dry-faced emoji. Then... *I'll go easy on them and get their rooms ready. ROOMS, as in plural!*

Ezra just smiled and texted her back a laughing face.

Once they were in the SUV, both kids in the back seat, he glanced at the two of them in the rearview. Emma had her head laying on Lucas's shoulder, her eyes closed, and Lucas was looking down at her as if she hung the moon.

Ooooh, Ezra knew that look. Yeah, Lucas wouldn't stay put if they told him to. He was too close to being old enough to move out on his own and he loved this girl.

"Is Berlin, ah..."

"Mad?" Ezra supplied. "She's not happy with you. And she's really into revenge."

At that, Emma sat up slightly. "What?"

"Since you're under eighteen she might give you a pass." Ezra kept his voice neutral as he resisted the urge to laugh. "But she's been known to shave heads or put Nair in people's shampoo if 'they've angered the goddess.' Her words, not mine. In some cases, she's cleaned out people's bank accounts."

Lucas's eyes narrowed. "You're messing with me."

Ezra grinned as he pulled up to a stoplight. "I'm pretty sure she's done all those things, but yeah, she'd never do that to you. But you did break her trust and it'll take time to earn it back."

Lucas groaned. "I just didn't want Emma to be alone."

"Oh god, your mom is going to hate me." Emma looked pained.

"No she won't," Ezra said before Lucas could respond. "*You* didn't do anything wrong. Lucas should have told his mom what was going on. None of this is on you."

"I thought it would be easier to ask for forgiveness." Lucas half grinned, but Ezra could see the hint of worry on his face as he glanced at him in the rearview.

"Maybe. But if you break someone's trust enough times, it gets harder and harder to earn it back." Ezra turned the radio up slightly, left it on the holiday station as he headed back. He figured that was a good note to end on anyway.

***

Magnolia had plates and glasses set out for the kids as they arrived. Even though she'd been swimming in fear that something had happened to Lucas, she was glad Ezra had been the one to pick him up and not her.

She'd had time to have an actual reaction and not overreact in front of her son's girlfriend. Because at the end of the day, she never wanted to be like her own father. He'd judged Ezra without getting to know him. And while she'd never be a "cool mom," she still wanted to have a relationship with anyone that Lucas brought home.

"I'm sorry I snuck out." Lucas pulled her into a hug the moment he, Emma and Ezra stepped into the kitchen. "I just hated the thought of Emma being alone. I wasn't trying to break your trust."

"It's my fault, Ms. Lavigne." Emma stepped forward, the girl Lucas had told her about looking impossibly young in that moment. "He only snuck out because I asked him to."

"None of this is your fault. And I'm sorry that you've been on your own. We'll make sure someone picks up your car and brings it here or to my house for a bit. Are you guys hungry?" Because food fixed everything.

Emma looked at Lucas and the two had a silent conversation before they both nodded.

Aaand that was that. She fed her son, his girlfriend, then showed them to their separate rooms before making her way to Ezra's room.

He was already in bed, sans shirt because clearly he was trying to give her a heart attack. "You know they're going to end up in the same room, right?" His tone was dry.

"I'm choosing not to think about that at all." She stayed where she was, leaning against the closed door. Because if she got any closer, she'd end up in bed with him. And she wasn't a glutton for punishment, thank you very much. He'd already rejected her Christmas invitation. "I'm so angry at that sweet girl's mom for just abandoning her." She hadn't wanted to say much because of Ezra's own history, but they were eventually going to have to do something.

"Yeah, me too."

"I'm about to get some sleep but I wanted to thank you for how you handled things with Lucas. It helped having time to figure out how to react." The last thing she wanted to do was push her son away.

"Of course." He cleared his throat and sat up slightly and there was something in his expression she couldn't read.

So she opened the door, needing an escape. Because keeping things platonic between them was killing her. Yes, yes, it was probably the smart thing to do, but emotions she thought she'd buried, or at least managed to get a handle on years ago, were all bubbling to the surface. "I'll see you in the morning." She was out of his room, shutting the door behind herself before he could respond.

CHAPTER 29

It's okay if you fall apart sometimes. Tacos fall apart and we still love them.

"Thank you again for letting me stay here. I know you guys have a lot going on right now." Emma was soft-spoken and she had a sweet demeanor.

"You don't have to thank me again," Magnolia said, smiling at her before she turned back to the stove. "I hate that you've been on your own."

"It's not a big deal." There was a hint of maybe defensiveness in her tone. "I can take care of myself."

Oooh, so she wasn't going to touch on that subject, at least for now. "I hear you're quite the actress. Lucas says that you're amazing on stage." She glanced over her shoulder again and found Emma smiling, her cheeks pink.

"I don't know about amazing, but I love it up there. I'm not good enough to do it forever, for like a job, but it's been a lot of fun."

"I hear you're also working while going to school. That's impressive." She slid the last chocolate chip pancake on the plate, then set one in front of Emma. "Take as many as you want."

"Thank you. And yeah, I'm just hostessing some evenings. When I turn eighteen, I want to wait tables. That's where the real money is at. I figure I can do that and go to school, at least part-time."

"Where are you looking at?"

"Hopefully Tulane. It's really expensive but I've started looking at scholarship opportunities and there are a lot I can apply for. We'll see." She snapped her mouth closed, then shrugged again, her cheeks turning even pinker as if she worried she'd said too much.

"Two of my hotels work with Tulane. We offer paid internships and on-the-job experience for hospitality. But we also offer the same thing for people who aren't interested in getting their undergrad and just want to start working right away. There are pros to each option. So whatever direction you decide to go, if you're interested let me know and I can put you in contact with the right people."

Her eyes widened slightly. "Seriously?"

"Absolutely."

"Thank you. I will."

They also offered scholarships but Magnolia figured she'd already dropped a lot of information on the girl.

Emma continued. "And I can get out of here this morning—"

Magnolia shook her head. "Nope. Unless you have to work today, you can stay here with Lucas."

Emma looked relieved as she cut into her pancakes. "I don't work today. Normally I do work Wednesday and Thursday evenings but I took this week off since..." She cleared her throat. "Since Lucas just got out of school for break. We wanted to spend some time together."

Ah, young love. Magnolia smiled at her, then glanced down as her phone buzzed across the countertop. Her heart kicked up at Camila's name.

"Hey, any news?" Magnolia asked as she stepped outside onto the back patio. She didn't think Camila would be calling this early without a purpose.

"We got him. Freaking nailed the bastard." She could hear the glee in her friend's voice. "He's asked for a lawyer but it's not going to matter. Not after the stunt he pulled with the truck. He caused so much damage, not to mention all his other crimes. I'm going to try to get him to confess to shooting at you and the bombing, but either way he won't be getting out on bail. If he does, I'll let you know, but I don't think it'll happen. Not with how brazen that attack was, combined with his current warrant."

For the first time in days—heck, weeks, since she'd been dealing with the threatening messages for longer—true relief punched through her, making her light-headed. She sat on one of the chairs, her knees basically giving out from euphoria. "That's great news, thank you."

"I'm just glad to be able to give you some news at all. You can enjoy your Christmas break now with that sweet boy of yours."

"That sweet boy has a girlfriend and is going to be a man soon." Seriously, when had he gotten so grown? She looked through the windows from the patio, saw that Lucas and Ezra were now in the kitchen, piling food onto their plates.

"What? When did that happen?"

"Oh, I'll tell you later. I'm not actually sure how long they've been together, but she's cute as a button and seems really sweet. And he's definitely in love," she whispered the last part, and wasn't sure why.

Lies. She knew why—her mama's heart wasn't ready for all this.

"Okay, you, me and Mari are setting up a girls' date and catching up."

"Deal. And I better see you at the Christmas Eve party." She was throwing a party this year on the twenty-third since most of their friends had family stuff on the twenty-fourth but she was still calling it a Christmas Eve party.

"Absolutely. So…is Lucas's father going to be at the party?"

"I haven't actually asked him." She *had* asked him over for Christmas, but he'd been weird about it.

"You should. I know some of the people he works with—you've probably met them over the last few days."

"Uh yeah, I have."

"Ask them too!"

She narrowed her gaze even though Camila couldn't see her. "Why so pushy?"

"Because I want to know more about them. I'm a *detective*, I can't help it."

"I'll invite them but you're not grilling anyone."

"Fine. Okay, the asshole's lawyer is here so I've gotta go. But I'll touch base later. Oh, I called his ex-wife, let her know that Perry has been found and arrested. She's ecstatic. Talk soon."

Emotions battled inside her as she tucked her phone away. Relief, elation, exhaustion. Wait, was exhaustion an emotion? *Hmm*. As she stepped back inside, she said, "Perry's been caught. Camila just called. He's got a lawyer, but Camila doesn't think he'll get bail, not with how brazen his last attack was."

Lucas looked up from shoveling in his pancake. "That's awesome. Does that mean we can go home?"

"Yep."

She saw the panicked look on her son's face so she kept going. "And Emma, I'd like to ask you to stay with us for the next few days at least until we can figure some things out. We have a couple guest rooms and we'll pick up your car so you've got transportation."

"Yes," Lucas said before Emma could answer. But he trailed off as he looked at her. "I mean, right?"

Cheeks pink, she nodded and smiled.

Magnolia was definitely going to have to figure something out—and had a plan for what she was going to do—but the next few days at their place would be fine. "Good, it's settled, then. When you guys are done eating, why don't you go pack up your stuff? I'll grab the dishes."

They hurried out of the kitchen, Lucas taking a pancake in hand because of course he did.

"I'll help you clean up this place before we head out," she said to Ezra who was pouring a mug of coffee.

He hadn't said anything yet, which surprised her. "I don't know if you should go back home just yet," he finally murmured, his whiskey voice doing what it always did.

Making her weak in the knees.

"Why not?" Frowning, she started putting the plates in the dishwasher.

"I don't think it would hurt to play things safe for a little longer."

"If he gets out on bail, then we'll come back here, but we know it was him. He left his cell phone at that guy's place and then he tried to ram us in broad daylight and got caught on camera. And Berlin found those texts that basically admitted to the bombing."

"Someone added mushroom powder to those brownies." They knew that from the testing. There had been definite traces of mushroom powder.

"Yes, but Berlin looked up that gift basket set online and brownies are part of it. If Perry had wanted to poison me, that's a smart way to do it. It's not like it would have hurt anyone else who ate them, unless of course they had an allergy too." And they had no idea who'd sent the gift basket either. They'd assumed it was a client. This time of year they got a gift basket every other day from clients or vendors and they were piling up in the break room, most missing any sort of notes. She'd finally told people to start taking some of the stuff home because there was no way they'd be able to eat it all.

"I still don't like it."

"I don't like any of this, but we can't stay here forever. We have to get back to our lives." One she really hoped he wanted to be part of.

She could tell he wanted to argue, but Ezra finally nodded, then said, "You don't have to clean up anything. We call someone each time we use this place."

"Okay..." She suddenly felt awkward standing in the kitchen with him with nothing to do or hold on to. So she grabbed another mug of coffee even though she was way past her caffeine intake for the day (a full pot was a bit much, but whatever). "So, we're having a Christmas Eve party on the twenty-third. I know you were kind of iffy for Christmas, but if you want to come, we'd love to have you. It's very casual and fun."

Once again he got that almost panicked look. And it was like he shoved that metaphorical blade between her ribs once again.

She sighed and set her mug in the sink because she didn't need more coffee. "Ezra, you don't have to come. And I was inviting you to a party, not a beheading."

"I know, I just want to keep things..."

"Friendly?" she supplied when he couldn't seem to find the right word. Because she was pretty certain there wasn't a good word for his bullshit. She bit back a sigh this time. "Well the invite is out there if you'd like. And it's clear that you're trying to put up some walls or boundaries, I'm not sure, but I'll respect them. I hope you call Lucas and set up some times to visit him. You both deserve to get to know one another and I hope you end up having a relationship with him." But at the end of the day, she couldn't force it. That was up to him.

Ezra scrubbed a hand over his face. "I'm just trying to keep boundaries for myself. Because I never got over you!" He practically hurled the last few words almost in accusation.

She stared at him in confusion. "You never got over me so you want to keep your distance from me now that I'm not in danger? How does that make sense?"

"We would never work out, and then what happens? I'm out in the cold with Lucas and I lose him too."

"Okay so we can't even work out as friends?" she demanded.

"That's not what I'm saying."

"That's exactly what you're saying. And you know what, it's bullshit. Everything right now is bullshit!" And she was done. Just emotionally done with everything right now.

"Magnolia—"

"No. I'm done with this conversation. But for the record, I never got over you either. So we're clearly in the same boat, but you're too afraid to see if there's anything still there." She let out a laugh that sounded bitter to her own ears. "Hell, there *is* something still there as the other night proved. But you keep your distance, you coward. I'm going to pack." She stomped out of the room, probably childishly, but she didn't care.

And as soon as she hit the top of the stairs, she called Mari.

"Hey, I heard the good news from Camila already," Mari said by way of greeting.

"Hey...I need a ride. And my best friend."

"Tell me where you are and I'll be there."

Chapter 30

Magnolia looked up at the half knock on her office door, managed a tired smile for Charles. Mari had picked up her, Lucas and Emma and taken them home while Ezra had asked someone to drop off Emma's car. So all that was settled.

Unfortunately nothing else was settled inside her, even with the knowledge that Perry was currently in jail. So she'd come to work to give Lucas and Emma some space, and truthfully, to get her own emotions in check.

"Hey." She managed a small smile. "I didn't realize you were still here." It was six and everyone had left an hour ago.

"Had a few emails to catch up on." He gave a half smile. "I'm about to head out though, wanted to check on you."

"I'm good and about to get out of here myself." She wanted to go home, get in her pajamas and have a pity party.

He nodded, cleared his throat. "Listen, I did want to talk to you about something and wanted to wait until it was just the two of us."

"Sure." She nodded to one of the seats in front of her desk. "What's up?"

"If we get the Gray job, I want to take lead. I've got the most experience and I picked up all the slack on the West End project."

Oooh, she really didn't want to have this conversation. But she was the boss so she had to. "I actually want you as PM on the Sinclair job. You've already got a working relationship with the owner and he *loves* working with you. It makes more sense for you to take on that job, especially since it's going to start right after Christmas. The Gray job might not start until February and that's even if we get it."

He gritted his teeth. "We're going to get it."

"Maybe." And the truth was, in no part because of him. He'd dropped the ball with Tremblay and even though it had worked out, he hadn't been pulling his weight. Not where it was needed.

"Is this because of Tremblay?" he finally asked.

"No."

He raised an eyebrow.

"Okay, partially. But it's definitely not the only reason. You're really great with the custom jobs."

"The small ones," he practically spat.

"Smaller, yes, but still important to our company. We're diversified for a reason. And you've been killing it the last year."

She'd almost let him go a year ago but he'd turned things around. But he still wasn't ready for a huge job because she couldn't micromanage. Hell, she didn't *want* to, but she had to trust her employees a hundred percent. And she didn't with him.

"You should have been able to land Tremblay," she continued when he didn't say anything. "And I'm not going to harp on it, mainly because we're going in a better direction. We're lucky to have landed someone so talented. But if we hadn't landed someone new, you should have been able to get Tremblay to sign with us. I think Davids is better suited for the Gray project—if we even get it." Though at this point, she and everyone else were feeling really good about their odds.

"She's only got a bachelor's degree." He said it with a certain amount of disdain that got her hackles up.

But Magnolia kept her expression neutral. "Yeah, but she's also got eight years' experience and...she's got incredible soft skills. The kind that can't be taught. She's great with people, handles stress better than anyone here. And for a job this size, I need someone cool under pressure."

Sighing, he stood. "I've been offered a job at the Lawson firm. As a senior project manager."

Magnolia nodded, stood and plucked up her bag. She'd actually heard he'd been putting out feelers, but hadn't been certain he was seriously job searching. "Are you going to take it?"

He blinked in surprise. "You're not..."

"Angry? No. I'd never stand in the way, and I think you'll do a great job for them." They were a smaller firm and worked with a certain type of clientele (ahem, good ole boys, of which her cousin was a part). And that was part of the problem with him—he worked well with people from the same tax bracket as him, people who looked like him, but he could be classist. And she didn't want that in her employees. He was giving her a great out right now and she was going to take it.

He shoved out a sigh. "Wow, I thought you'd, I don't know—"

"Look, this is a business. I understand that you have to make the right decision for yourself. If you want to put your official notice in, let's do it now. You can simply enjoy the holidays and take the time to reset before you start your new job. And we'll pay you out for your accrued PTO. You can get your personal stuff later. It's getting late so just check back in tomorrow if you want."

Looking a little shell-shocked, he nodded and headed out. She waited until he was gone before she ducked back into her office and pulled up the list of keycards and deactivated his.

Then she deactivated all his logins and sent off a message to their IT person to let them know what she'd done. She didn't think he'd do anything shady, but she'd been burned during her first year as owner so it was second nature to do it now.

Ugh, this might make Christmas dinner awkward, but it was what it was. After closing down, she headed out for the second time, and froze when she saw her SUV.

All four tires were flat. As she stepped closer, ice chilled her veins. They'd been slashed.

Cold snaked down her spine as she looked around, but of course the gated parking lot was empty. Even though she didn't want to, she called Ezra.

To her surprise, he answered on the first ring. "Hey. Everything okay?"

"Ah...my tires have been slashed." And now she was wondering what the hell was going on. Because Perry couldn't have done it.

"Stay where you are. I'm just down the street." He disconnected before she could respond.

Even as she wondered why he was so close, she let herself out of the parking lot and headed to the curb, her heart rate kicking up as she saw him in the distance. He hadn't been kidding, he was close.

As he pulled up in front of her, a truck across the street squealed away and she saw Austin Jameson tearing down the street.

What the heck was going on?

CHAPTER 31

"We should wait for the police. Something I never thought I'd say," Ezra murmured.

"No. I'm texting Camila right now. She's in with Perry, but I've given her the gate code. I'm done with all this and waiting around will accomplish nothing. She can take pictures and dust for fingerprints or whatever without me." Magnolia simply wanted to get home to her son. "I'm also reaching out to our IT department..." She trailed off as she composed another text asking them to pull security footage from the last few hours. No doubt the police would want it, and she did too.

Ezra steered away from the curb, his jaw tight, but at least he didn't push back. She hadn't even wanted to call him, but she was shaken, *frightened*. She'd been so relieved to have Perry locked up but now... A shudder rolled through her.

Ezra called Berlin using the SUV's Bluetooth system.

"Heya," she said, slightly out of breath. "What's up?"

"Someone slashed Magnolia's tires at work. Are you still logged into her security?"

"Ah, yeah. Let me pull it up." She was silent for a long moment, then... "Huh. About an hour ago someone inputs the code at the gate, walks in, then quickly slashes the tires. They're wearing a hooded, bulky jacket. It all happens fast and whoever it is knows exactly where the cameras are."

"Man or woman."

"Man. Or a very large woman, but body language and shoe style suggest a man."

"Send it to me and Magnolia. She's already reached out to Detective Flores. It might not do any good, but they can add it to their file."

"All right. I'm going to see if I can track this person using other cameras, try to get a face."

"Austin Jameson was hanging outside her office when I picked her up so focus on him."

"Will do. By the way, have you decided to pull your head out of your ass with her and—"

Ezra quickly hung up, smashing his finger against the dashboard screen.

"I knew I liked her," Magnolia murmured, not bothering to hide her snicker. "So why were you so close to my office?" She groaned as he pulled up to a red light. Great, traffic had decided to be a major jerk tonight of all nights.

"I wanted to talk to you."

"You...could have called me."

He sighed and she tried not to look at him, even as she wondered if he'd intentionally rolled the sleeves of his shirt up to his elbows to show off his forearms. "I didn't want to bother you at the office."

"I hear a little bit of judgment in your voice right now."

"I didn't think you should have even gone to the office this afternoon, but I wasn't going to let you go without protection."

She wanted to argue with him but someone *had* just slashed her tires. Someone who couldn't be Samuel Perry. And fine, she sort of loved that he was so protective even if he was trying to protect her from him or whatever misguided crap he was thinking. As she started to answer, her phone rang.

When she saw her father's name on-screen, her finger hovered over the green button, but she ended up declining. Talking to him now wasn't the best move.

A moment later, her phone rang again, this time from her mom. "Hey, Mom."

"Hello, darling." Her mom's normally light voice had a slight edge to it. "Great news that the police found that monster."

"Ah yeah, really great." She decided not to tell her mom about her tires being slashed just yet. She wanted to see what the PD or Berlin could find. "Did you want to come over for dinner tonight? Lucas's girlfriend is staying with us for now and you can meet her. I'm making tacos." Her mom's favorite.

Her mother cleared her throat slightly. "Ah, not tonight, we've already eaten. But I did want to talk to you about something. Your father and I decided to take your advice and invest in that new parking lot construction but we had some questions and were hoping you could stop by and answer them. I know your friend Camila decided to invest as well so I'd like to hear her thoughts."

Ice slicked down her spine, but she answered. "Sure. I'm just headed home. I had some car issues but I've called for a ride. Can you drive me home afterward?"

"Of course, darling. See you soon."

"Something is wrong," Magnolia said as soon as her mom ended the phone call.

"What did she say?"

"It was weird. She turned down tacos, something she would never do. And she declined to meet Lucas's girlfriend, which she would definitely not do. But then she mentioned this investment opportunity one of their friends had asked them about. I advised against it, but she said she was taking my advice to invest. Then she mentioned Camila investing, but...Camila doesn't know anything about that as far as I know."

Ezra dialed Berlin back without responding. "Hey," he said when she picked up. "Log into Magnolia's parents' security system. See who's at their house and if something is going on." He made a right-hand turn at the next light in the direction of her parents.

"Yep, hold on." She was silent but Magnolia knew she was working hard. "Their system is offline completely. Their cameras too. I'm looking back to when it went offline..." She cursed slightly. "It's only been off twenty minutes. Before everything goes offline there's a short shot of someone in a bulky hooded jacket—the same one at Magnolia's office—knocking one of the cameras out with a baseball bat. Not long after, the system goes down completely."

Ezra cursed slightly. "Call the others, tell them to get there quickly. I'm with Magnolia and we're maybe seven minutes out. I'll park down the road and make a quiet entrance."

"On it now."

As Berlin hung up, he turned to Magnolia. "Contact Camila and let her know what's going on. But no sirens."

With trembling hands, she dialed her friend, but Camila didn't answer so Magnolia texted her to let her know the situation. Then she called Lucas and nearly cried when he answered.

"Hey, Mom. Are you almost home?"

"Hey, hon. I'm currently dealing with something but I need you to do something for me. Can you set the alarm and make sure all the doors are locked? Then I want you to go upstairs into the game room and lock the door."

"What's going on?" he asked even as she heard the security system arm in the background.

"Honestly I'm not sure right now but I just want you to stay safe while I figure it out. Don't answer the door for anyone. Okay?"

"Okay. Emma and I are heading upstairs now. I'll keep my phone on me. Is Ezra with you?"

"He's right next to me."

"Okay, good. Be safe and please keep me updated."

"I will. I love you."

"I love you too."

Sighing, she set the phone in her lap and turned to Ezra. "What's the plan?"

CHAPTER 32

"You're not going with me." Ezra slid his jacket on, zipped it all the way up as he glanced down the quiet street. He'd parked only a block away, underneath an oak tree with limbs extending over half the street.

"Well I can't just sit here and do nothing."

"All I'm doing is recon to see what's going on. It sounds like your mom is under duress, likely your father too. I need to see who and what I'm up against."

"Your team is twenty minutes out."

"Yeah and by the time they get here, I'll know what's going on. I'll be fine." He tucked a pistol in the back of his jacket as he shut the door behind him and stepped onto the curb. Then he slid his earpiece in. "Call my phone."

She did as he said, then he pressed the answer button.

He shut the back hatch of the SUV as he said, "Testing, can you hear me?"

"I can hear you."

"Okay. I'm on my way." There was so much he wanted to say to her, but every time he tried or thought he had a hold on things, the words got jumbled up in his head. They were both silent as he jogged down the sidewalk.

The neighborhood was all lit up with Christmas cheer, with a few cars driving by, but no one stopped to look at lights or him, it seemed.

When he reached the driveway to her parents' house, he kept going, then hurried down the neighbor's driveway. He knew this was a risk, but if the neighbors called the cops on a potential intruder, then there was nothing he could do. "I'm using the neighbor's yard as cover. Sticking to the shadows," he murmured.

"Which neighbor?" Magnolia asked.

"One on the left side if you're looking at their house from the street."

"It's Wednesday so...you should be good. They go to Wednesday and Saturday Mass almost every week."

He picked up the pace, racing down the line of hedges until he neared the back boundary between their yards. "There's one car in the driveway. A dark green Land Rover." One he recognized.

"Oh god."

"Yeah," Ezra gritted out, coming to the same conclusion as her. "I'm moving to the backyard, going quiet for a minute."

"Okay."

He hoisted himself up and over, glad the neighbor's backyard didn't seem to have any sensor lights, or at least not near the fence line. He was silent as he moved across their backyard, sticking to the shadows of trees. From the back, their house was dark except for one window. So he moved up to it, but could only make out shadows behind the gauzy curtains.

Someone, a man, was standing near a fireplace. Then two others, one he was certain was Magnolia's mother, were sitting on chairs as the man paced, his actions jerky. Ezra texted Magnolia instead of risking speaking.

"Can you hear me?" she asked.

He texted back *yes*.

"Okay, I have an idea." He heard the SUV engine flare to life, had to bite back his order as she continued. "I'm headed your way.

He eased back from the window, kept his voice low. "Wait, no, stay where you are. I'm going to sneak in."

"No. I'm just going to pull into the driveway and call my mom and ask her to come out and help me with something in the trunk. I'll pop it and then stay out of sight. If he comes outside, you take him down."

"That is...not a bad idea. Do you have the pistol I gave you?"

"I've got bear spray courtesy of Mari. She gave me a canister yesterday, called it an early Christmas present. Have you seen my parents? Do they look okay?"

"They're alive." They'd been moving, but he couldn't see more than that. "How close are you?"

"Two houses down."

"Okay, give me a minute to get into place," he whispered as he approached the back door. "I'm at a back door. Tell me what I'm walking into."

"It's a sort of entryway. To the immediate left is a butler's pantry and then that opens up into the kitchen."

He worked quickly on the lock using one of his kits. "What's to the left of the kitchen? I saw them sitting in a room with a fireplace."

"That's my dad's study."

"I'm in so I might not be able to respond."

"Okay, I'm pulling into the driveway now. I'll stay closer to the road and pop the trunk then make the call."

"After you pop the trunk, head for the neighbor's yard and get out of sight when you call. I don't want him to see you at all or for you to be in the line of fire."

"Okay. I'm hanging up so I can call."

After she disconnected, he felt the loss as if she'd physically cut the connection between them, even though that was nonsensical. Or maybe it wasn't because he'd been trying to keep walls between them, to save himself in case... In case what? Jesus, he wasn't sure what was wrong with him.

Okay, lies, he knew. He was terrified of going for it again with her, then losing her. But not having her at all, not giving them a shot, was even more terrifying. And he felt the loss of what he was giving up all the way to his core.

Which is great timing, really.

As he moved through the kitchen on silent feet, he could hear a phone ringing in the distance.

"When I press the green button, you better talk normally to her!" an angry male voice snarled.

Ezra moved through the kitchen, closer to the voices. He stepped into a small hallway, could see light coming out from underneath a closed door a few doors down.

"Oh, hello darling."

"Hey, Mom." Magnolia's voice slightly carried, so he guessed she was on speaker. "I'm here. I've got a few bags I need help with. Would you come out and help me carry them?"

"Oh, ah...of course, of course. I'll be out in a moment, love you."

"Why the hell did you say that?" Another angry snarl.

"It would be weird if I said no," her mother snapped. "And you haven't done anything you can't take back."

"Just shut up and let me think! Okay, okay...okay, I'll head out and help her. Then when I get back in here, we're going to have a nice little chat, all of us."

"No—"

At the sound of a slap against skin, Ezra took a deep breath, dug for control. Right now he had to do things right. He called Magnolia back, but she didn't answer. *Shit.*

When he heard the sound of the door opening, he ducked into the nearest dark room with the door open. A bathroom.

Footsteps moved in the opposite direction so he stepped back out, moving quickly. He ducked into the study, held a finger to his mouth when he saw Abigail and Arnold tied to two chairs. Arnold was groggy, one eye swollen and bloody, his nose broken. Abigail looked mostly unharmed except for a red mark on her face. There was also a wall safe open, empty. He catalogued everything in seconds as he moved.

Ezra hurried to her tied arms, freed one and handed her his knife. "I have to follow him and keep Magnolia safe." Then he raced back out, his steps quiet as he followed in the same direction as the clomping boots.

He peered out into a living room, could see the front door starting to swing closed so he sprinted, racing through the living room and catching the door before it fully shut.

Pistol up, he eased it open to see Charles striding down the walkway on un-steady feet. The SUV trunk was popped open, but at this angle it was impossible to see who'd popped it.

Charles paused, his weapon held down by his side. A heavy-duty pistol that would tear someone apart. Maybe he sensed Ezra or sensed that the situation was off.

Either way, it was the end of the road for him. Ezra raised his SIG. "Put your gun down, Charles, then raise your hands and lie on the ground. It's over."

Charles froze, his body vibrating with rage as he stood there trembling. "You have no idea what I'm dealing with," the man snarled, desperation clear in his voice. He took another step away from Ezra.

And Ezra wasn't going to shoot someone in the back unless absolutely neces-sary.

Ezra moved after him. "Whatever you're dealing with, you know Magnolia will help."

Ooh, that had been the wrong thing to say. "She fired me today!"

That...didn't sound accurate.

"Stupid bitch. She just doesn't understand," he continued his rant as he reached the end of the curved walkway onto the driveway.

Ezra stepped into the yard instead of following after him, wanting to cut him off before he could head toward the road.

That was when he saw the cluster of carolers strolling down the sidewalk. *Oh, shit.*

Charles saw them at the same time, raised his gun in the air and started firing upward.

Screams rent the air and the carolers scattered in all different directions. Charles dove into the hedges by the driveway and there was no way Ezra could risk hitting someone else.

He gave chase, racing down the driveway and rounding the hedges at the same time a gunshot rent the air. Once, twice, each sound an explosion.

On instinct he went down to one knee, aimed at Charles who was waving his pistol around wildly. Ezra pulled the trigger, nailed him in the chest.

Charles stumbled backward and everything seemed to happen in slow motion. Out of the corner of his eye he spotted Magnolia hiding behind the neighbor's tree, bear spray in hand.

Charles fell to his knees, his eyes wild and manic, and he was still clutching his weapon.

He tried to raise it again, but Ezra fired again, hitting him directly in the chest. Charles flew back, landing at an awkward angle, not moving.

Ezra moved toward him, kicked the weapon out of the way even as he stumbled himself. Pain registered in his chest as he struggled to draw in a breath. At least Charles was incapacitated. Permanently.

"Ah, shit," he rasped out, falling to one knee.

Sirens sounded in the background so at least someone had called for backup.

Suddenly Magnolia was leaning over him, her eyes filled with tears. "No, no, no!" she shouted. "You're not going to die because I'm too mad at you. You're going to be just fine!"

"Why are you mad at me?" he rasped out, pain lancing through his chest.

Whatever she was going to say, her voice broke on a sob.

Until he unzipped his jacket, knocked on his bulletproof vest, then groaned in pain. That had been a dumb thing to do. "Think he broke a rib. But I'm...okay." He just felt like someone had taken a hammer and decided to play the drums with it on his chest.

She clasped his cheeks even as the sirens grew louder. "Oh god, you really are okay. I love you, you big dumbass. And I'm always going to want more from you."

"Same. But you're not a dumbass. You're wonderful." Even though it hurt to breathe, he forced the words out. "And I love you so much it hurts. I never moved on from you and...I haven't been handling my emotions well, according to my friends. I thought... I don't know what I thought. But I want to be more than friends with you. I want everything—the whole deal."

"Ezra—"

"Ma'am, I'm going to need you to move out of the way." Suddenly an EMT was there, nudging her to the side, then kicking Ezra's SIG into the grass.

"She rides with me," Ezra rasped out, aware of his crew showing up. He could see Tiago arguing with a uniformed police officer. "And her father needs help way more than me. He's next door. He was roughed up."

"We've got more than one ambulance," the man said as he popped the gurney up. "Another team is with him right now."

"Well, I'm fine. I don't even need—"

"You're not fine and you're going to do everything this man says," Magnolia snapped, clasping onto his hand tightly with both of hers. She basically bared her teeth at the EMT who tried to get her to move so the guy worked around her and got him into the back of the waiting ambulance.

He really was fine. Just really, really sore and yeah, okay, it hurt to breathe. He would just close his eyes for a moment.

CHAPTER 33

One word can change a person's day from bad to amazing. Tacos.

Two days later

Ezra was stretched out in the recliner in Magnolia's living room—she'd bought it especially for him and had it delivered while he was in the hospital—and debating how hard it would be to get out of this dumb chair without help. As soon as he was healed, he was burning the damn thing.

Rib fractures were the absolute worst because there was nothing he could do about it. Just heal and suffer silently.

The front door opened, then closed, and he heard multiple footsteps in the foyer before Magnolia, Berlin, Mari, and Detective Flores...Camila stepped into view. She must have arrived at the same time as the other three because they'd been at his place, packing up some personal stuff for him.

"Hey," Magnolia said, moving right to his side. "How are you feeling?"

"Eh."

She winced and dropped a quick kiss on his forehead—his *forehead*. Another shitty side effect of this stupid injury. Magnolia was treating him as if he was made of glass. Little pecks on his mouth, cheek and yes, forehead.

Just kill me now, he internally groaned.

"We packed up some stuff from your condo." Berlin put a bag down while Mari set a suitcase next to it.

"Your condo makes me sad," Mari added. "It's gorgeous, but..." Mari shook her head, which made Berlin devolve into laughter, as if they'd already had a conversation about his place.

He frowned, looking between the two of them. "Are you two friends now?"

"They bring out the twelve-year-old in each other." Magnolia's tone was dry, but he could see her fighting a smile.

Camila sat on the edge of the couch, looking exhausted but happy. "Why don't you two make some coffee or something?" she said to Mari and Berlin, who disappeared down the hall toward the kitchen. Then she looked at Ezra, her expression softer. "Rib injuries suck."

"Yeah. So, what do you have?" Because he didn't think this was a social call.

"We've finally wrapped up everything and I just wanted to assure you that you're one hundred percent off the hook for shooting Charles Barbier. The case has been closed as clear self-defense and the DA will not be pressing charges, blah, blah blah. I'm sure you already knew that, but I wanted it clear."

He nodded, because yeah, he'd known. He'd already gotten a call about it. "Thanks."

"I also wanted to let you both know that Samuel Perry is pleading guilty to the drive-by shooting, most of the threatening messages the last couple weeks and of course the attack in broad daylight with the stolen truck. Barbier was the one behind the poisoning." Camila looked at Magnolia then. "We've found enough evidence at his place and after an electronic audit of all his belongings and what your parents have told us to paint a clear picture of what was going on. He'd been trying to sabotage your recent bid. He'd been working with a man named Louis Tremblay."

"Bastard," Magnolia muttered.

"It doesn't seem that he was involved in any of the nasty stuff, just the corporate espionage side. When you snagged Tabitha Johnson, Charles saw everything crumbling around him. And I'm extrapolating from some of his text messages and emails. Then when he threatened to quit and you didn't stop him, but encouraged him, according to what he ranted to your mother, he snapped. He owes a lot of really scary people money."

"How much money?"

"Half a million."

Magnolia blinked in surprise and even Ezra was shocked by the number.

"It was partially from bad investments and a gambling addiction. His normal bookies cut him off so he went to some people I can only tell you are really, really nasty."

"Are they going to be a problem for us?" Ezra asked.

Camila shook her head. "I doubt it but we'll be keeping an eye on them in case. But no, you're not on their radar. And after the attack on your parents and you, they're going to stay far away from you."

Ezra knew some of that as well, since Abigail Lavigne had stopped by earlier this morning to check on both of them. She'd looked exhausted and about to break.

"So he used the threat of Perry as, like, a cover to threaten me? To...almost kill me?" Magnolia asked, shock in her voice.

Ezra gently squeezed her hand for support.

"It looks like it. We think he was behind the attempted bombing at your house, not Perry. If you were dead, that job would have likely gone away, or the bid would have been postponed. And since Austin Jameson is the next real option for the bid, your cousin knew the job would go to him. Or assumed."

"You haven't mentioned Jameson until now. He was outside Magnolia's work Wednesday evening." Which felt like a lifetime ago. "Has anyone talked to him?" Ezra asked.

Camila nodded. "I did, personally. He said he stopped by to apologize in person for his behavior at her office a few days ago. He said he tried calling but apparently her assistant has him on her 'asshole list' and Magnolia wasn't returning his calls."

Magnolia nodded in agreement.

"Was he involved in any of this?"

"I honestly don't think so. There's no trail leading back to him. Just something Tremblay and your cousin cooked up. If Tremblay ended up getting the position as architect working with Jameson, he'd planned to use it to his advantage. He's always had a certain amount of sway in suggesting which contractors to use. And one of those is—"

"Connected to one of those nasty people you were talking about?" Ezra's tone was dry.

"Bingo. And Charles planned to leave Magnolia's company in a big 'screw you' to her once she lost the contract and all those nasty people got work for their company. From what we can tell, he was killing two birds with one stone. He wanted to screw over Magnolia, who he thought was holding him back, and pay off the debts he owed all at once. In the end, this was all about money and not a little bit of misogyny. At least that's what it looks like from my end."

Camila shook her head in disgust as she continued. "And for the record, Jameson is cutting ties with Tremblay. He was pissed when I laid out everything for him. I think Tremblay will lose a lot of business—I don't know enough about your industry, but I do know New Orleans. He's going to be blacklisted." Camila stood, clearly wrapping things up. "I just wanted to tell you both in person that there's no threat and you can enjoy your Christmas break. Also, I'll be at the party next week."

"You'd better." Magnolia pulled Camila into a big hug.

Once Camila had left, Ezra said, "I hope I'm still invited to the party. And to Christmas."

Magnolia gave him a surprised look as she sat back down next to him, scooting her chair up to the recliner. "I wasn't planning on letting you leave the house. If you tried, I was going to duct tape you right here."

He laughed lightly, winced.

"Ack, sorry."

"Don't apologize. If anything, I should be apologizing to you. I tried to explain but I know I sounded like an asshole."

"You had just been shot." Fear flickered into her blue eyes for a moment, but she shook it off.

"I was...scared. Scared of losing you, but then I was losing you anyway. I don't know where I fit into your world, or Lucas's world, but I want to figure it out. I want to make up for lost time. I want to create a real life with you, Magnolia. I love you. I know I've said it, but I'm going to keep saying it."

"I love you too," she whispered. Tears glittered in her eyes as she leaned forward, kissed him hard.

He bit back the sting of pain as he shifted slightly, cupped the back of her head and returned her kiss with equal fervor. He'd waited almost two decades for this woman. A little pain was nothing.

CHAPTER 34

If you don't like where you are, move. You're not a tree.

December 23ʳᵈ

Magnolia slid her arm around Ezra, oh so gently, as she stood next to him around the bonfire in her backyard.

The party was in full swing, with people congregating around the finger foods and cocktails in the kitchen, some in her living room singing Christmas karaoke, and Ezra and most of his friends out by the bonfire talking, drinking and laughing.

This was probably the biggest Christmas Eve party she'd thrown and was definitely her favorite, since Ezra was here.

"How are you feeling?" she murmured, leaning up to kiss him.

"Perfect." His voice was pitched low as he brushed his lips over her mouth, then the top of her head.

"Liar."

"I've got a couple more hours in me."

"Well don't overdo it. As soon as you're ready, I'll grab some ice and you can sit."

"I'm lucky to have you." The deep timbre of his voice rolled over her as he leaned in even closer.

"You definitely are." That was from Tiago, who had his arm around his fiancée, Fleur, an artist Magnolia was a fan of. And now friends with.

"So what are you doing with that condo anyway?" Mari, who'd quickly become friends with all of Ezra's crew, asked. "Because I know someone in the market."

"I think I'm going to keep it," Ezra said. "Rent it out or maybe Lucas can use it when he goes to college."

Magnolia blinked in surprise. She hadn't even realized he'd thought about those things. "Really?"

"Absolutely."

She wanted to kiss him senseless now, but simply smiled up at him and wished they were all alone and he was completely healed. Because she wanted to do all sorts of things to him right now that involved them being naked. And from the heated look in his whiskey gaze, he was thinking the same thing. They'd recently found out that she'd had the wrong address years ago when she'd sent him those letters and it had settled something in her knowing for sure what had happened. And in him too, she thought. Life had seen fit to tear them apart before, but never again.

"Oh god, you two, get a room." This was from Bradford, a man who'd flown in to celebrate Christmas with all of them. He was currently staying at Magnolia's house and she found she really liked him.

"Shut it," Ezra growled, then winced slightly. It was so subtle she wasn't sure anyone else saw it, but she realized he needed to sit.

"We're going to head inside and mingle, but I expect all of you to go one round of Christmas karaoke. The winner gets the big prize."

"Come on, we'll do a duet and destroy everyone." Mari winked at Magnolia as she linked arms with Berlin and dragged her inside against her protests.

Magnolia was so happy that Mari had found a friend in Berlin, that she'd seamlessly integrated into Ezra's found family. She wasn't sure if he even realized it, but he had a family with them. Knowing that he hadn't been alone while she'd had Lucas eased the ache when she thought about all the time they'd missed together.

In the kitchen she found Lucas and Emma with all the other young people clustered around the dessert table as they piled food onto their plates. Lucas was proudly wearing the silly birthday crown Emma had made for him, even a day after his birthday—her kid really was in love.

Emma was currently living with Camila and finishing out her high school year. After that, who knew what would happen, but her life was stable, she had a safe place to lay her head at night, and lived with a guardian who adored her. And Camila had made it clear that Emma didn't have to move out the moment she turned eighteen, that she could stay as long as she wanted. That was all Magnolia could hope for.

She bypassed the living room and pulled Ezra into her small home office/study and shut the door, immediately shutting out fifty percent of the noise.

"What's up?" he murmured, pulling her into a loose hold.

She didn't squeeze him, ever mindful of his healing injury, but she gently laid her face against his chest. "Just wanted a moment with you." Then she looked up at him as she found the courage to ask what she'd been wanting to. "So if you're not going to be using your condo..."

"I was hoping I could move in here." He looked nervous as he said the words.

"You basically already have." She'd talked about it with Lucas and asked if he was okay with it, and her son had looked surprised she'd even asked. He already loved Ezra and liked having him around.

"While I've been healing."

"Well I'd planned to simply move you in completely and hope that you stayed," she said, only partially joking. Things were still new, yet not between them. They had so much history, and she tried to tell herself to slow down but the wild part of her didn't want to. The part of her that had missed so many years with him wanted to dive in head—or heart—first and just go for everything she'd always wanted.

"Good, because I wasn't planning on moving out," he murmured as he took her left hand in his—and slid a diamond ring on her ring finger. "Also, I was hoping to wait a couple months but clearly I have no self-control where you're concerned. Marry me?"

"Yes," she whispered, looking at the ring in awe, then back up at him, her heart so full her entire chest ached with the pressure of it. Almost losing him, after just getting him back, had made her terrified that this was all a dream.

"Soon?" he continued as he peppered kisses along her jaw, slowly working his hand under her bright red sweater.

She moaned slightly as he pushed her bra out of the way, then his other found its way up under her long skirt. "We can't do anything right now." She was too worried about him hurting himself even as he began teasing his fingers between her legs.

"I just want to get you off...and you still haven't answered me." His voice was ragged as he palmed her breast while simultaneously sliding his finger over her clit.

"Yes, as soon as you want," she rasped out as he gently pinched her already hardening nipple. She'd agree to anything at this point. She'd been so careful with him the last week-plus, not wanting to hurt him.

"One month. Maybe two," he growled against her mouth. "You're going to be my wife."

"Yes, yes." She'd agree to anything as he began rubbing her clit in a tight little pattern.

And as he slid a finger inside her, she was grateful she had incredible insulation in her office as he gave her an early Christmas present. One that almost rivaled his other present that would link them together in every way.

EPILOGUE

Two months later

Ezra finished tightening Lucas's bow tie and was actively fighting all the emotions that wanted to spill over. "You look great," he rasped out as he took in his son in a tux, standing next to Tiago, Rowan and Bradford. They'd been his "boys" since he was eighteen and now he had a new one, and oh shit, he couldn't cry.

"You really do." Tiago clapped him once on the shoulder. "You're gonna show up your old man for the big day."

Lucas full-on grinned and casually did that thing where he dusted off his shoulders. "I can't help it."

Violet, the wedding planner, stuck her head in and was, as always, the epitome of calm. "Ezra, I need you. Well, the bride needs you, so chop-chop."

"I feel like she needs German subtitles," Bradford muttered, making the others laugh.

Violet looked at the others, her gaze narrowing on Bradford. "You four, get in place now."

As his friends all straightened, Ezra headed for the door. He hadn't wanted to jinx things before the wedding by seeing Magnolia in her dress, but if she needed him, he was going to be there.

"We'll see you on the other side, Dad." Lucas called out as he eyed himself in the full-length mirror, still messing with his tie.

Ezra blinked and met Lucas's gaze in the mirror.

His son grinned and turned away from his reflection. In that moment, he was all Magnolia. "I'm trying something new out. I like it."

"I do too." Aaand he was definitely going to cry.

As a man who'd cried twice in his entire life that he remembered (which according to Magnolia was *not* healthy) he couldn't get a handle on his emotions today.

"Is everything okay?" he asked Violet as she ushered him down the hall, her heels making angry-sounding clicks.

The last two months he, Magnolia and Lucas had gotten into a routine, one he loved. He didn't even feel like he was figuring out his place in their lives, he was simply part of it now. And that realization had nearly bowled him over as much as Lucas calling him dad all casually only moments ago.

And even though things between Magnolia and her father were still rocky, the man was in their lives. He'd apologized, sincerely, more than once after Ezra had saved his and Abigail's lives. And while Ezra didn't think he'd ever throw back beers with the guy, he was willing to move forward, albeit cautiously. Now he was worried that something had happened.

"Of course everything's fine." Apparently that was all the answer he was going to get before she knocked on the door at the end of the hallway and poked her head in. Then she nodded at Ezra to go in.

Magnolia was standing by a window of the historical building that had once been a speakeasy but was now a venue for all sorts of events. In a lilac gown covered in soft little sparkles that glittered in the light, she was a walking dream. Her dark hair was down in soft waves and—

"Hey, what's wrong?" He was moving before he realized it at the expression on her face. "Whatever it is, we can fix it." He didn't care where they got married, as long as they were together. Gathering her in his arms, he held her close, loving the way she fit perfectly against him.

Her blue eyes were brighter today, probably because of the dress color, as she looked up at him. She set her palms on his chest. "I need to tell you something and I should have told you before this morning, but I've been all up in my head. And I feel like such a fool that I've waited so long and I've built everything up—"

"I know you're pregnant. If that's what you want to tell me."

Her mouth parted slightly. "You do?"

"You switched to decaf a couple weeks ago."

She blinked once. Twice. "Oh. Are you...okay with this?"

"I'm thrilled." He tightened his grip slightly. Though thrilled wasn't the right word. How about over the moon?

"Why didn't you say anything?" she whispered.

"I thought you just needed time to tell me and things were so perfect between us I... I don't know. I talked to my stupid therapist—"

"Not stupid," she murmured, almost on instinct, her mouth curving up into a smile.

"Fine. My annoyingly insightful therapist brought up that the last time you told me, or tried to tell me, I disappeared. So maybe you were simply being cautious, even subconsciously." Stupid, absolutely brilliant therapist that she'd insisted he talk to.

"Wow, okay, she's not wrong. Every time I tried to tell you, the words got caught in my throat. Because you're right, things have been perfect and this is a huge change."

He hugged her even closer. "A change I'm ready for. I missed the first time around and I'm excited about this. I want to be there for you for everything. Also, Lucas just called me dad for the first time."

Magnolia's eyes filled up with tears so he quickly swiped them away. "Mari said you weren't allowed to cry until after pictures," he murmured.

Making Magnolia laugh. "That sounds about right."

"Okay, so we're ready to get married? No more secrets? Because I love you more than life itself, and I want to call you my wife."

Smiling as bright as the sun, she kissed him, then nodded against his mouth. "I love you too. Let's go do this, my soon-to-be husband."

Even though they weren't supposed to, they walked down the aisle together, because screw tradition. He'd waited too long to claim her and he wasn't going to be separated from her another second.

Dear Readers

If you'd like to stay in touch and be the first to learn about new releases you can:

Check out my website for book news: https://www.katiereus.com

Also, please consider leaving a review at one of your favorite online retailers. It's a great way to help other readers discover new books and I appreciate all reviews.

Happy reading,
Katie

ACKNOWLEDGMENTS

As always, I'm so thankful to Sarah for all the things, a list too long to attempt. I'm also thankful to Julia for helping me get this book in shape. To Book Nook Nuts, thank you for beta reading. To Shelley and Tammy, who often send me notes letting me know about typos, thank you from the bottom of my heart! To Jaycee, I love all the covers in this series and this one is no exception! Thank you for always working with me. For my mom, who won't even see this, thank you for all you do. I'm eternally grateful. For Piper and Jack, the greatest writer pups, thank you for keeping me company every day and reminding me to get out in the sunlight. I'm also incredibly grateful to all the strong women in my life who have helped shape who I am today. Every single one of you. And for my readers, you guys are incredible. Thank you for reading my books, talking about them, reviewing them... thank you for everything.

ABOUT THE AUTHOR

Katie Reus is the *USA Today* bestselling author of the Red Stone Security series, the Ancients Rising series and the Redemption Harbor series. She fell in love with romance at a young age thanks to books she pilfered from her mom's stash. Years later she loves reading romance almost as much as she loves writing it.

However, she didn't always know she wanted to be a writer. After changing majors many times, she finally graduated summa cum laude with a degree in psychology. Not long after that she discovered a new love. Writing. She now spends her days writing paranormal romance and sexy romantic suspense.

COMPLETE BOOKLIST

Sentinel of Darkness

A Very Dragon Christmas

Darkness Rising

Deadly Ops Series

Targeted

Bound to Danger

Chasing Danger

Shattered Duty

Edge of Danger

A Covert Affair

Endgame Trilogy

Bishop's Knight

Bishop's Queen

Bishop's Endgame

Holiday With a Hitman Series

How the Hitman Stole Christmas

A Very Merry Hitman

MacArthur Family Series

Falling for Irish

Unintended Target

Saving Sienna

Moon Shifter Series

Alpha Instinct

Lover's Instinct

Primal Possession

Mating Instinct

His Untamed Desire

Avenger's Heat

Hunter Reborn

Protective Instinct

Dark Protector

A Mate for Christmas

O'Connor Family Series

Merry Christmas, Baby

Tease Me, Baby

It's Me Again, Baby

Mistletoe Me, Baby

Red Stone Security Series®

No One to Trust

Danger Next Door

Fatal Deception

Miami, Mistletoe & Murder

His to Protect

Breaking Her Rules

Protecting His Witness

Sinful Seduction

Under His Protection

Deadly Fallout

Sworn to Protect

Secret Obsession

Love Thy Enemy

Dangerous Protector

Lethal Game

Secret Enemy

Saving Danger

Guarding Her

Deadly Protector

Danger Rising

Protecting Rebel

Redemption Harbor® Series

Resurrection

Savage Rising

Dangerous Witness

Innocent Target

Hunting Danger

Covert Games

Chasing Vengeance

Redemption Harbor® Security

Fighting for Hailey

Fighting for Reese

Fighting for Adalyn

Fighting for Magnolia

Fighting for Berlin

Sin City Series (the Serafina)

First Surrender

Sensual Surrender

Sweetest Surrender

Dangerous Surrender

Deadly Surrender

Verona Bay Series

Dark Memento

Deadly Past

Silent Protector

Linked books
Retribution

Tempting Danger

Non-series Romantic Suspense
Running From the Past

Dangerous Secrets

Killer Secrets

Deadly Obsession

Danger in Paradise

His Secret Past

The Trouble with Rylee

Falling for Nola

Tempted by Her Neighbor

Paranormal Romance
Destined Mate

Protector's Mate

A Jaguar's Kiss

Tempting the Jaguar

Enemy Mine

Heart of the Jaguar